Labyrinth of the

Maiden to the Dragon, Book 3

Mac Flynn

All names, places, and events depicted in this book are fictional and products of the author's imagination.

No part of this publication may be reproduced, stored in a retrieval system, converted to another format, or transmitted in any form without explicit, written permission from the publisher of this work. For information regarding redistribution or to contact the author, write to the publisher at the following address.

Crescent Moon Studios, Inc.
P.O. Box 117
Riverside, WA 98849

Website: www.macflynn.com
Email: mac@macflynn.com

ISBN / EAN-13: 9781791892920

Copyright © 2018 by Mac Flynn

First Edition

CONTENTS

Chapter 1..1
Chapter 2..9
Chapter 3..16
Chapter 4..21
Chapter 5..29
Chapter 6..36
Chapter 7..42
Chapter 8..48
Chapter 9..55
Chapter 10..63
Chapter 11..69
Chapter 12..75
Chapter 13..81
Chapter 14..88
Chapter 15..95
Chapter 16..102
Chapter 17..109
Chapter 18..116
Chapter 19..121
Chapter 2..127

Continue the adventure................................134
Other series by Mac Flynn............................142

LABYRINTH OF THE DRAGON

CHAPTER 1

"Are we there yet?"

Regrettably, the whine came from me, but I had to blame my butt. After eight days of travel it was hanging by a thread to what was left of my jostled spine.

"Nearly there," Xander assured me.

I glanced around at the scenery and our shrunken party. Cayden and Stephanie had separated from us after we exited through the southern part of Viridi Silva. The scenery had changed with their passing. Gone were the vast expanses of rolling, tree-covered hills of the High Castle and woods, and in their place was a landscape of short stony mountains and small glens. Winding strips of trees broke the landscape and signaled that one of dozens of smalls creek supplied water to the cottages that dotted the hills. The water ended at small ponds where farm animals lapped up the precious resource.

"So what's going to happen when we do get to this city of yours?" I asked him.

He smiled. "You will be presented as my Maiden before my people and trained in your responsibilities."

I raised an eyebrow. "What responsibilities?"

"As Maiden to me, you are queen of my kingdom. You will manage the palace and address any problems that arise therein," he explained.

The color drained from my face. "Run the palace? I haven't even run a business."

Xander chuckled. "Do not feel anxious. Darda and many others will assist you."

The road we traveled was a wide, hard-packed dirt way. We passed many carts as they rolled along in the same direction as our little group. Many of the drivers pulled to the side of the road and bowed their heads at Xander. He smiled and returned the gesture.

"So does everybody know what you look like?" I asked him.

He shook his head. "No, but they are aware only those of my house are allowed to bear the crest of my family."

"And how many people *are* in your house?"

"It is only I who remain of the main branch, but I have a family of distant cousins who I have granted use of the coat. Unfortunately, you are little likely to see them for they do not reside in the city, but live abroad."

My face fell. "That sounds kind of lonely."

Xander smiled. "My duties keep me preoccupied. Do you have any siblings?"

I shook my head. "No, but there's my parents. They're divorced, but I still see both of them."

He arched an eyebrow. "'Divorced?'"

LABYRINTH OF THE DRAGON

"Yeah. Don't you guys get divorces over here?" I wondered.

"What does it mean?"

"Well, it means they're not married anymore," I explained to him.

Xander furrowed his brow. "We do not have that custom here. If one marries, they marry for life."

I snorted. "That means you dragon lords take a big risk on the Maidens, don't you? You could be stuck with someone you don't like."

He smiled at me. "I am grateful I will not have to consider this 'divorce.'"

I shifted in my saddle and winced. "Speaking of divorces, my butt's about to divorce itself from the rest of me. How far is it?"

Xander nodded at a long, gentle slope in front of us. "Alexandria is just over that hill."

I craned my neck as we climbed the hill and peeked over the ridge. There, laid out on a small plain, was the city of Alexandria. The metropolis abutted a large lake fed by the snow-capped mountains to its northwest. The late morning sun in the east cast a dazzling glow on the white stone buildings with their timbered and shingled roofs. Steeples pierced the skyline, and a large square opened in the very center of the grid. The whole of the city was protected by a tall stone wall fifty feet high and half as thick. A single wide gate allowed entrance into the city.

The lake was nearly round with an active harbor filled with dozens of docks large and small. Sailing ships were anchored near the harbor, and smaller boats littered the docks. A small island sat some hundred yards out and was connected to the mainland by a narrow strip of land. Trees covered its otherwise rocky shore, and I could see a large white obelisk near the far shore with a small stone building situated at its base.

The palace of my dragon lord was a majestic fortress of white stone situated along the northwest shore of the lake. It had four terraces that climbed halfway up the steep, white-stoned mountain. A gate at the bottom-most terrace had fifty feet of lake-front property before a long dock stretched out into the waters in the direction of the city.

Xander paused and studied me. "What do you think of it?"

"Wow," I breathed.

He chuckled. "I am glad to hear you say so."

I swallowed my amazement and nodded at the castle. "That must be pretty easy to defend."

"In six thousand years, it has never been taken by outside forces," he told me.

I arched an eyebrow. "What about inside ones?"

He pursed his lips and tugged on the reins of his steed. "Unfortunately, my family has not been immune to internal strife. But come. I am eager to see my home from a closer distance."

We carried on and in a half hour had reached the gate. The archway towered thirty feet above our heads, and the two wood doors, made of six-inch thick boards nailed together with metal bands, were twenty feet wide. They were thrown open to the many carts, wagons and pedestrians that streamed in and out of the gate.

Three guards on either side had their backs to the arch and watched all who came and went. There was a small wood door in the left pillar of the arch. The guards noticed our regal group and stood at greater attention. Spiros rode up to the doorway and dismounted. The guard closest to the door knocked on the entrance.

A man stepped out and looked around. He wore the armor of a soldier but with a crooked, ragged felt cap on his head of shocking red hair. Perched on his shoulder was a small, gray-and-white hawk with alert yellow eyes.

Spiros smiled as the man saluted him. "How goes, captain?"

A crooked smile slipped onto the man's lips and he saluted Spiros. "Better now that you're back, Spiros You can take the blame for my mistakes."

Spiros cleared his throat and jerked his head over his shoulder. The captain looked past him at us. His face fell and straightened a little more before he bowed. "Greetings, My Lord!"

His proclamation caught the attention of everyone around us. The pedestrians stepped back and gawked while the cart drivers hurried past to make room.

Xander smiled and bowed to him. "Greetings, Kinos. I see the city still stands."

Kinos nodded. "It does, My Lord, but she shimmers now that you have returned."

Xander turned his horse toward the long street in front of us. "I shall make the inspection myself, and if I should find a blemish I will give you the lash."

"Spare some for my commander, now that he has returned," Kinos added with a sly look at Spiros.

"I will do so," Xander agreed, and with a bow of their heads we headed off. Spiros jumped onto his horse and followed behind.

I leaned toward Xander. "Who was that?"

"Kokinos is the captain of the city," he told me.

I glanced over my shoulder at Spiros. "Isn't Spiros in charge of that?"

Xander shook his head. "No. Spiros leads the castle guards and my personal retinue, and Kokinos does report to Spiros."

"But you called him something else. Kino?" I guessed.

He smiled. "Kinos is merely a nickname. His true name is Kokinos."

"And does that mean anything?"

"It refers to the color red in the ancient Alexandrian language. Kinos's family is legendary for their hair."

I looked around us at the broad cobblestone street. On either side were two-story houses made of dried brick, some with open shops for their bottom floor and others used completely for housing. Their walls were whitewashed to perfection and many had flower pots beside their wood doorways. Chimneys puffed out smoke from kitchen stoves and warmed the streets with wondrous smells. Over many of the doorways were carved a sword of stone.

However, I couldn't help but notice the many stares we received. People stepped aside and bowed to us. The travelers in their cloaks gawked at our presence. Children leaned out their windows and waved to us. Some of them peeked out far enough for a necklace to dangle out from their necks. On the end of the jewelry was the same sword design as over the houses.

"So is this how much attention all your walks through town get?" I asked him.

"And sometimes a great deal more," he replied.

I shrank beneath all those staring eyes and curious faces. The main road traveled through the large city square I had seen from the hill. An enormous fountain with three tiers sat in the center. Covered stalls lined around the perimeter of the circular square and people hawked wears of all kinds. There were fabrics, fruits, furniture, and small animals.

One small animal was familiar, and over our heads. A white hawk flew over us in the direction of the castle. I pointed at the bird. "Isn't that-"

"Kinos's own hawk. He takes news of our arrival to the castle," Xander explained to me.

"I wish it'd take me. . ." I mumbled.

We rode through the square and back down the main street to the docks. The bustle of activity wasn't slowed by our arrival. Crews loaded and unloaded boxes, crates, and all sorts of smaller objects and officials with clipboards made tallies of the wares coming and going.

Our retinue rode to the longest and most pristine dock in the whole of the harbor. It stretched into the water for two hundred feet, and tied to one of the tall posts was an elegant sailing ship. The ship was fifty feet long and half that distance wide. Its shimmering wooden masts matched the white sheets of its sails. At the head of its bow was a mermaid with a naked upper torso and a fish tail.

The deck and dock had a tough-looking crew with patched clothes and a few of them with scars on their arms and faces. One of them was a scraggly fellow with an eye-patch and a grizzled gray beard.

He waved a finger at one of the crew on deck, a man in a clean outfit. "Watch yerself there, sir! Keep your wits about you!"

The man sneered and waved his hand. "Ah knows, sir, Ah knows!" He picked up a wood box and walked to the gangplank. His foot slipped on a puddle of water and he crashed onto his rear.

The grizzled man shook his head and glanced in our direction. He squinted his eyes for a moment and a smile broke through his whiskers. "Well, well, look what the land rats brought to us."

Xander dismounted and the rest of us followed suit. "Good day, Captain Magnus. I hope the winds are favorable."

The captain limped over to us and nodded his head. "The winds are always temperamental, Yer Lordship, but today they are smiling on ye." His eyes fell on me and his bushy gray eyebrows shot up. "What have we hear? Has Yer Lordship caught his fish of the sea?"

Xander half turned and gestured to me. "Captain Magnus Heinason, allow me to introduce you to my Maiden, Miriam Cait."

The captain bowed his head. "It's a pleasure to meet ya, My Lady. His Lordship's caught a fine fish, a very fine fish."

Xander nodded at the ship. "Is she sea-worthy, Captain?"

Magnus followed his gaze and grinned. "Aye, but for some landed fish on the crew. Some of me sailors went and abandoned ship for a better port at Bruin Bay, but I say 'bah' to them! None good pickings of ladies there, the fools!" His eyes flickered to me and he coughed into his hand. "That is, none good work to be got there, Yer Lordship."

"May we board, Captain?" Xander asked him.

The captain stepped aside and swept his hand to the ship. "Of course, Yer Lordship, of course! Come aboard, ye and all yer men!"

CHAPTER 2

Our horses were led away to a stable situated along the harbor and we were led onto the ship. The crew scurried out of our way and up the rigging to set the sails. Xander and I moved to the railing while the captain took his place at the wheel. The sails were unfurled and the captain let out a laugh as they were filled with a soft, but steady wind.

"See that, Yer Lordship! Even the winds want to see you home!"

"I must give thanks to the god of the winds!" Xander replied.

The length of the dock allowed the ship to turn full around and face the castle beyond the lake. We moved to within a few hundred yards of the island with its natural bridge.

I nodded at the little kingdom unto itself. "What's that?"

Xander's eyes flitted to me as a mischievous smile slipped onto his lips. "A shrine to the fae of the lake. The merchants raised the temple over two thousand years ago so the fae would grant them good waters. They still care for the grounds to this day." He leaned close to me and lowered his voice. "Perhaps you would introduce them to your relation."

I looked down into the deep, dark water and shuddered. "I think I'll pass."

Xander nodded at the way ahead of us. "Will you pass on such a home?"

I followed his gaze and looked in wonder at the majestic white castle. The shimmering clean glass of its numerous large windows twinkled as though winking at us. A small crowd awaited us at the dock, and the hawk flew over us screeching in glee.

Our ship docked and we climbed down the gangplank. The leader of the crowd stepped out. My face fell when I recognized Renner, Xander's personal adviser and the man who least wanted me to be Xander's Maiden. He'd been left behind at the High Castle to deal with some duties. I wish he'd stayed there a bit longer, like maybe a decade.

Renner spread his arms open and hurried up to Xander. "My Lord! It is good to see you well! We feared the worst when our party reached the city before yours, but a hawk from King Thorontur assured us you were well and would arrive soon."

Xander grasped his adviser's eager hands and smiled. "We could not leave a friend who was in need of our help, but tell me the news of the kingdom."

LABYRINTH OF THE DRAGON

Renner nodded and the pair turned their backs on me as they walked toward the tall gates of the castle. They were as large as those that protected the city. I followed them up the gentle incline and through the gates into the massive courtyard. It made the ruined castle of Pimeys look like a playpen.

The entire castle was hewn from the rock of the mountain on which it climbed. On either side of us were high walls with narrow glass window. The wall in front of us had larger windows, and rose up only half the height as the other sides until a parapet interrupted its progression. That tier drew back closer to the mountain and rose up until it, too, was interrupted by another wide walkway. The castle continued its climb until it rose so high my neck ached to look at it. At the very peak was a towering steeple with a tip that glistened in the midday sun.

"You were very brave to meet such a terrifying evil," Renner commented as he led Xander to the far back wall. "Several trades have arrived seeking permission to begin business, a message came from the priests of the south congratulating you on your Maiden success, and. . ." His yammering toddled off into more chatter that I couldn't catch.

I made to continue my shadowing of them, but Darda grasped my shoulder. She nodded at a smaller door in the left of the rear wall. "If you would follow me, My Lady, we will suitably dress you."

I blinked at her. "We're gonna do what?"

She nodded at my clothes. "My Lady cannot wear such attire in the city. She would attract attention."

"What if I wore something over it?" I suggested.

She shook her head and tugged me to the left. "That will not do, My Lady. Please come with me and we will get you fitted for some wonderful clothes."

I tugged back. "I'd really just like to keep my-"

"My Lord would be very pleased to see you in them," she pointed out.

I pursed my lips. "Because this is part of being his Maiden?"

She nodded. "It is, My Lady."

My shoulders sagged. "All right, but no needles. I hate needles."

There were needles. Lots and lots of needles. The seamstress used them to pin the cloth together as she draped me in a variety of bright colors. Darda had led me into the castle's white stone halls and up a flight of stairs to the women's quarters, a wing separated from the other parts of the castle by the lack of doors leading to any other part.

So there I was a few minutes later in one of the chambers given to me atop a stool covered in silky, tickling cloth. My arms had been stretched out for so long I thought they were going to fall off and walk away. I wanted to join them.

The seamstress stepped back and studied me. The diabolical woman with needles shook her head. "My Lady, I cannot fathom your color."

"How about white?" I suggested.

She arched an eyebrow. "Are you fond of white?"

I shook my head. "Not really, but I'll blend in great with the walls around here."

"My Lady, please focus," the seamstress scolded me.

LABYRINTH OF THE DRAGON

My eyes focused on Darda who stood a little ways off. *Save me* I mouthed. She shook her head and pressed a finger to her lips. I was on my own.

"Ah-ha!" the seamstress exclaimed. She rushed to me and tore off most of the fabric. Pins and needles flew everywhere. Two young girls who acted as assistants flitted down and scooped up the fallen pointy objects.

Soon I was left with only one color stuck to me. Blue.

The seamstress stepped back and clapped her hands together. "Beautiful! Magnificent! You look marvelous!"

I looked down at myself. The scrap of cloth was barely a foot square and was pinned to my chest. "Please get this off me."

The seamstress snatched the cloth from my chest and admired the deep blue color. "You are a special woman, My Lady. Very few who have your dark hair may wear this color, but the color suits your pale skin to perfection."

"I'm not that pale," I commented as I looked down at my arms. They were a little paler than I remembered.

"My Lady is very modest, but I will get to work on your wardrobe immediately!" she promised as she swept to the door with her two girls behind her.

"Does that mean I can drop my arms now?" I asked her.

She paused at the door and bowed her head. "Of course, My Lady. Good day to you, My Lady." And with that the strange crew flitted out.

I dropped my arms and stepped off the stool. "Is anybody normal in this world. . ." I murmured as I rubbed one of my sore shoulders.

"Miss Raptis means well, My Lady, and she is the finest seamstress in all the city," Darda defended her.

I looked down at my ragged modern clothes. "You don't think I could get her to make a couple more pairs of jeans, do you?"

"You would have no occasion to wear them here, My Lady," Darda pointed out.

I pursed my lips and looked around the room. The area was a small chamber that was connected to a bedroom and sitting room. I approached the windows and looked out on the courtyard some twenty feet below us. These rooms were in the corner on the first tier. The hallways ran against the wall of the mountain and were lit with the same small lights I'd seen at the fae city.

"So what do I do?" I wondered.

Darda came up behind me. "Beg your pardon, My Lady?"

I turned and gestured to the room around us. "What do I *do* here? Do I just sit around in fine clothes sipping wine?"

Darda smiled and shook her head. "No, My Lady. As Maiden to the lord of Alexandria you are required to maintain the castle and all its grounds, though not the docks."

"So do I need to start making a grocery list for all these people?" I suggested.

She chuckled. "No, My Lady. The cook handles all those arrangements."

"And who pays all these clothes I'm going to be buying?"

"The exchequer chancellor will handle your bills, My Lady."

"Do I need to pick up a broom and get sweeping?"

"There are servants who will provide the cleaning services."

I threw up my arms. "So what do I do?"

"They will report to you of their activities, and you will give approval over any questioned decisions," she told me.

My face fell. "That sounds like I'm the scapegoat for the big stuff."

"Only if a mistake is made, My Lady."

I turned around and grasped the windowsill. This was sounding like a really bad idea. A commotion below us caught my attention. A group of soldiers hurried through the gates and into the courtyard. People shouted and I saw Xander emerge from the main doors.

I spun around and, with a smile on my face, hurried to the door. "Finally some action!"

"My Lady!" Darda yelped as she followed after me.

CHAPTER 3

I raced down the flights of stairs and out into the courtyard. Darda was just exiting the door when I reached the group of people. The new soldiers, four in all, were lined up in front of Xander and Renner. Close on Xander's other side stood Spiros.

"What is the meaning of this?" Renner shrieked.

One of the soldiers stepped forward and bowed to them. "I am sorry for this intrusion, My Lord, but we bring tidings from the southern border."

"What have you for me?" Xander asked him.

The soldier raised his head and looked the lord in the eyes. "There has been another attack on the colonies there, My Lord. Two have been destroyed."

A dark cloud overshadowed Xander's face. "The Bestia Draconis?"

The man nodded. "Yes, My Lord. We received the hawk only a half hour ago. The survivors have been taken in by the Southern Priests, and we may garner more information from them."

Xander turned to Spiros. "Inform the troops to meet me at the gate. I will go myself to see this destruction and learn what we can."

"B-but My Lord, you only just arrived!" Renner pointed out.

"A lord does not place his needs above those of his people," Xander scolded him.

I stepped forward. "Then as their Lady I'm going, too."

Xander turned to me and a ghost of a smile slipped onto his lips. "There will be more riding."

I winced, but resumed my stance. "I'm still going."

Renner leaned toward Xander and lowered his voice. "My Lord, your Maiden must remain here to provide the people with a pillar of strength. Otherwise, panic may ensue."

Xander pursed his lips. "Panic?"

Renner nodded. "Yes, My Lord. Once news reaches everyone of the attack, they will fear the same may happen to Alexandria. With your leadership absent from the city, there must be someone to guide the people."

I glared at the skinny little weasel. "How in the world am I supposed to do that?"

Renner turned to me and smiled. "With me by your side, My Lady, you will not be wanting for counsel."

I narrowed my eyes. "Who said I'd take it?"

Renner frowned, but Xander stepped between us. "We do not have the luxury to waste time on squabbling, but my

Maiden is correct. She has little experience and the people do not know her."

Renner bowed his head to Xander. "True words, My Lord, but the memory of your late mother still lingers over the city. She was beloved by all, and is still fondly thought of by your people. I thought perhaps your Maiden would likewise be respected."

Xander sighed, but nodded. "You are correct, Renner. Miriam, you will remain here and await my return."

My eyebrows crashed down. "But I can help, remember? I'm a not just a normal human-"

"You will remain here, and there will be no more argument about the matter," Xander commanded me.

He strode past me with his dog Renner close at his heels. Spiros cast a look of regret at me before he, too, followed Xander to the gates. I stiffened my upper lip and marched after them as they exited the castle.

Their heavy boots clapped on the dock as they approached the ship. I reached out and grabbed Xander's arm to turn him around. He furrowed his brow. "I told you the-"

"I know, the matter's closed and you're going off to be the big hero for your people," I interrupted him. "But I want you to promise me something."

He bowed his head. "Anything."

"Promise me you'll be careful. No heroics or anything stupid like that, okay?"

Xander raised his head and his soft smile shone down on me. "You make it very difficult for me to be both lord and husband."

"Well, I'm not ready to be a widow just yet, so you be careful," I insisted.

LABYRINTH OF THE DRAGON

My dragon lord leaned down and pressed a light, teasing kiss upon my lips. He drew back and met my blushing gaze. "I promise to be careful."

"Are ya boarding or not?" Captain Magnus called from the deck of the ship.

Xander straightened, stepped back and bowed to me. "Ever your servant, my Maiden. We will meet again soon."

My dragon lord turned around and, with Spiros at his side, boarded the ship. The sails opened and the traitorous wind blew them away from the long dock. I walked to the end of the planks and watched the ship sail to the far end of the lake.

"My Lady?" I glanced over my shoulder and found Renner and Darda close behind me. A half dozen guards stood at attention behind them. It was Renner who spoke to me. He smiled and bowed his head. "My Lady should return to the castle before she catches cold."

I turned to face him and frowned. "It took me almost drowning to catch a cold. I don't think I'm going to get one just standing here."

"But Your Ladyship is fatigued from your journey, and such fatigue leads to health dangers," he argued. He clasped his hands together and his smile widened. "And I also have much for My Lady to do while Our Lord is away, and she will need her rest."

"*She* just wants to be left alone," I corrected him.

He stepped aside and gestured to the gates. "As you wish, but inside the castle where you will be safe." To emphasize his words, the guards broke into two groups of three and lined either side of the dock.

I frowned and marched past the physical display of diplomacy provided by Renner. Darda and he followed me, and behind them came the guards. We entered the castle where I stopped in the middle of the courtyard and winced when the gates slammed shut behind us.

Renner slipped in front of me and bowed his head. "I will see My Lady at supper, if it pleases you, and we will discuss your duties while His Lordship is away."

I narrowed my eyes. "Do I have a choice?"

He chuckled. "Of course, My Lady, but His Lordship would be most upset to learn you excused yourself from your duties."

I pursed my lips and my shoulders fell. "Fine. I'll see you at supper."

He bowed his head again. "I look forward to it, My Lady."

I didn't.

CHAPTER 4

Renner departed. The soldiers and others followed the weaselly adviser or dispersed to the far parts of the castle. I was left alone, and behind.

My energy drained out of me. My head fell. I bit my quivering lower lip and fought back tears. My hands balled into fists at my sides and I glared at the ground. "What a jerk."

"My Lady?" Darda called out as she slipped beside me.

I wiped my tears away with my sleeve and turned to her. "What am I really doing here, Darda? What's the point."

"You are here because the gods have ordained that you should be here," she replied.

I shook my head. "I don't know what kind of gods you have around here, but I think they're laughing at me."

She raised an eyebrow. "My Lady?"

I ran a hand through my hair and shook my head. "I've only been here for two hours, but I already feel so useless. Like I'm just a stupid doll who's going to be dressed up so I can give a yes or no to a question about what brooms to buy or what fish to serve."

"You will grow more confident in your duties and I am sure you will manage more of them in the future," she assured me.

"But I want to do something now. I just want to be of service. . .to-" My eyes widened and I snapped my fingers. I grasped Darda's shoulders and drew her over to the far corner of the courtyard near the side door. "Do you know where the Sus Tavi is?"

She furrowed her brow. "The Sus Tavi, My Lady? Why would you wish to go there?"

"Do you?"

She pursed her lips and nodded. "I do, My Lady."

"Good! I need you to take me there."

Darda started back. "Take you there? But you cannot leave the castle without Lord Renner's permission, nor without your new clothes."

I shook my head. "Never mind about the permission or the clothes. Just get me some servant stuff, maybe some of your suits, and we'll get going."

"But why there, My Lady?" she persisted.

I folded my arms across my chest and grinned. "Because if I'm going to be in charge here than I know just the guy who can give me a crash course in what this city is really like."

"But Lord Renner-"

"-is not the guy I want to be talking to. Didn't you watch any movies before you came over here?"

LABYRINTH OF THE DRAGON

She started back. "Well, yes, but that was-"

"Maybe you saw some movies where a weaselly little bad guy tries to control the heroine when the hero's gone?" I suggested.

"You don't mean to imply-"

"I'm not implying anything except that Renner's a weaselly little guy and this heroine isn't going to be controlled by anyone," I insisted. I stood straight and tried to look regal. "Now are you going to help me or do I have to swim to shore?"

She sighed, but I noticed the corners of her lips twitched up. "As you wish, My Lady, but we will not have an easy time reaching the city."

I jerked my thumb in the direction of the dock. "What can't we take the boat?"

"Lord Renner will be watching the ship and if he notices your boarding he will insist on your staying at the castle."

I winced. "So I'd better start warming up for my backstroke?"

Darda pursed her lips and swept her eyes over the area. She leaned toward me and lowered her voice. "I may perhaps have a way for you to reach the city, but you must return to your room."

I frowned. "Why?"

She grasped my arms and looked me in the eyes. "Trust me, My Lady. Return to your room and let me help you."

I smiled. "All right, but don't keep the lady of the city waiting."

We parted ways. I returned to my chambers and took a seat in a chair by one of the windows, but I couldn't relax.

My strained mind played the courtyard scene over again. The act with Xander and his leaving stuck with me. What he said about me staying rang true, but I still hated being left behind.

My heart sank and I clenched the tops of my jeans. I sighed and shook my head. "Barely over the threshold of our home and I'm already thinking about a divorce."

My ruminations on court proceedings were interrupted by a loud, rough knock on the door. I had enough time to stand before the door flew open and three men clomped into the room. By their clothes and body odors I could tell they were from the ship. Two of them carried a large wooden crate between them and dropped the heavy box on the floor five feet in front of me.

The third man shut the door behind them and strolled over. He was about thirty-five with a noon shadow on his face and a twinkle in his weary eyes. His skin was as pale as the belly of a fish and his nails were sharp to a point. The man swept his bandanna off his head, revealing a head of slicked-back short black hair, and bowed low to me.

He spoke in a deep, low voice that sent shivers up my spine. "Good day, My Lady." He raised his head and met my eyes. His were so blue they were almost transparent. "We have been asked to escort you to the ship."

I shakily smiled at him. "That's great, but how are you going to do that?"

The man swept his thin hand over the crate. "If you would please step into the crate we will carry you to the ship."

The other sailors opened the top and I cautiously stepped up to the box. The interior was dirty, but otherwise clean. My eyes flickered to the pale man. "Before I get into this thing, do you mind telling me who you are?"

LABYRINTH OF THE DRAGON

He smiled and bowed his head. The man pressed his lips tightly together when he smiled like he was hiding something in his mouth. "I am the first mate to Captain Magnus. I am called Nimeni."

"And you were sent by him?" I asked him.

He shook his head. "No, My Lady. We were sent by the orders of Darda."

I looked past them at the door. "So where's she?"

"She went to her room to fetch something, and will meet us on the boat," he explained to me.

I pursed my lips, but drew one leg over the side of the crate. "All right, but be gentle. I don't see any airbags in this thing."

"We will be as gentle as discretion allows," he replied.

I didn't like the way that sounded, but it was too late. I tucked myself into the small box and they shut the lid. We were both lifted off the ground and out the door. The slats that made up the old crate weren't tight, so I was able to view the world as it passed by.

We reached the courtyard before we were stopped by no less a personage than Renner himself. The adviser stepped in front of us. "What brings you into the castle, Nimeni?" At least he hadn't lied about his name.

"Orders from the captain, Lord Renner," Nimeni replied.

Renner frowned. "What orders? And when does the captain of the ship have command enough to order his men into the castle?"

"The captain requested onions from the kitchen, Lord Renner."

Renner arched an eyebrow. "That many?"

"He is fond of onions, but if you would like to see-" Nimeni nodded at the men who set me down with a hard plop that jarred every bone in my body.

Renner stepped back and sneered at the crate. "That won't be necessary. Carry on."

Nimeni bowed his head. "Your Lordship is most generous."

I was picked up again and we carried on our way. We arrived at the docks and I saw that the ship was once more on this side of the lake. The men carried me aboard and down the large hatch stairway to the hold below the deck. They set me down, more gently this time, and opened the top.

I climbed out and wiped cold sweat from my brow. "That was a close one."

Nimeni smiled his peculiar smile. "Not at all, My Lady. Renner is known to have a great personal dislike for onions."

A soft set of feet stepped down the stairs and Darda came into view. Under one arm she carried a wrapped bundle. She peered around in the semi-darkness of the hold. "My Lady?" she whispered.

"I'm here, or what's left of me," I replied as I popped my back.

She hurried down the stairs and over to us. The men bowed and left us alone. "I hope they were not too rough with you, My Lady."

I leaned my head to one side and cracked my neck. "I've been bounced harder from clubs, but where have you been?"

She held out the bundle. "Your clothes, My lady."

I took the bundle and met her gaze. "You know, you calling me that in the city is going to get us a lot of unwanted attention. How about you just stick with 'Miriam' and I'll go with Darda?"

Darda bowed her head. "As you wish, My-" I wagged a finger at her.

"None of that."

She smiled. "As you wish, Miriam."

"Good." I glanced up at the beams over our head. "Now when does this over-sized canoe shove off?"

"The captain must finish unloading a few more crates and they will be ready to sail again," she told me.

I plopped the lid back on the crate and hopped onto my impromptu seat. "So who'd you convince the captain to help us? And won't he get into trouble?"

"The captain is of much the same mind as you, M-Miriam," she explained as she moved to stand close beside me. "He, too, wishes for you to see the city and know its people."

I patted an empty spot on the lid beside me. "How about you hop up here and talk to me that way. I don't like people standing when I'm sitting."

Darda smiled and climbed onto the lid. "You are very kind, Miriam."

I shook my head. "No, I just don't like special treatment for myself. Makes me feel uncomfortable. Anyway, the captain won't get into too much trouble, will he?"

"He holds a strong dislike for Renner, and will be pleased to vex him in any way he can," she assured me.

I grinned. "Sounds like my kind of guy, and speaking of the knowing the city, I guess we'll start with the captain and his men. They don't look like a typical crew for a lord like Xander."

Darda chuckled. "My Lord is not a typical dragon lord, but I see what you mean about Captain Magnus. He and his crew were once pirates, but Xander defeated Magnus's fleet in a naval battle some twenty years ago. Rather than execute them, Xander offered them positions in his navy."

I arched an eyebrow. "He trusted a pirate?"

"Even a pirate's got to have some honor, My Lady."

CHAPTER 5

The gruff voice called from the hatch stairway. The devil himself limped down the stairs and over to our crate where he eyed us with his single eye. "And to serve under a man who outfoxed ya so well in battle is an honor indeed."

I shrank beneath his steady gaze and blushed. "I didn't mean to-"

"Of course ya did, and never lie about what ya meant. Does no one a service to be not knowing yerself," Captain Magnus scolded me. He leaned close to me. "Besides, that mate of yers has a good eye for choosing his allies."

I found an interesting spot on the floor so I wouldn't stare at the eye patch that covered his left eye. My mind went over all the allies and stopped on Renner. "I guess so."

He leaned away from me and grinned. "Ya can't fool me, My Lady." He tapped the side of the eye patch. "Yer wondering what's under here, ain't ya?"

I cringed. It was a matter of being careful what you wish for. "Sort of?"

The captain chuckled. "Then why not have a look-see?"

He raised the patch. I expected either a healthy eye or a hollow in his skull. On both counts I was wrong. In the hollow of his skull was a round ball. The orb pulsed with a soft blue light.

The bit of twinkle looked familiar. I furrowed my brow and pointed at the ball. "Isn't that a soul thingy?"

Magnus dropped the eye patch and hid the hollow. "A soul stone, My Lady. It's how yer mate knew Ah was one to be trusted."

I blinked at him. "How?"

"Because the fae don't give them things away by the shipload, My Lady, and ya can't force one out of 'em. No, this one-" he tapped the eye patch, "-this one was given to me by a mighty pleased fae after Ah rescued one of his boys from a greedy sus."

I shook my head. "I still don't follow. Why should you be trusted because you have a soul stone?"

Magnus straightened and frowned. "This ain't any old soul stone, My Lady. It was given to me by the king of the Mare Fae 'imself, Valtameri." He studied me with that careful gaze of his. "Ya should be well-acquainted with him, you being a Mare yerself."

I started back. "How'd you know?"

LABYRINTH OF THE DRAGON

He chuckled. "This stone isn't just fer looks, My Lady, just like that one in yer pocket ain't fer weighing down those strange pants of yers."

I fished in my pocket and pulled out the small vial with Thorontur's soul stone. "You could see it through my clothes?"

He nodded. "Aye, My Lady. Twas simple for me."

I narrowed my eyes. "What else can you see with that stone of yours?"

The captain held up a hand and shook his head. "None of what yer thinking, My Lady. This eye of mine only sees the magic in the world, not the whole of the world."

I gave him one last suspicious glance before I held up the vial in front of my face. "So can mine do that?"

"Ya can never tell until ya try," he told me.

I popped the cork and rolled the stone into my palm. "So how do I find out?" I asked him as I pocketed the vial.

Magnus tilted his head back and looked up at the beams over us. "Methinks Ah'll leave that lesson for when ya get back, My Lady. We're about to land, and you'll be wanting to change out of those strange clothes of yers."

"I'd rather know now," I insisted.

He half-turned away and gave me a wink over his shoulder. "It's best to be learning it yerself what yer stone can do for ya, My Lady. Enjoy the city. It's a fine place with the best of wine." He limped up the stairs and out of sight.

My face fell. "Some help he is."

"But he's right about the landing, Miriam," Darda spoke up as she opened the bundle of her spare clothes. "Now let's get you out of those clothes."

I was halfway through the undressing when we felt the ship dock, and nearly done when the gangplank clattered against the pier. I looked down at myself. The plain white blouse with long sleeves was tucked into a baggy tan skirt that reached to the ground. The cuffs were frilly things that covered the lower halves of my hands. My feet didn't fit into Darda's shoes, but the skirt would hide my modern sneakers.

Darda pulled my long hair back in two tails and tied them together into a tight, elegant braid. She stepped back and smiled at me as she gave a nod. "There. A finer servant girl I never saw but one."

I winced and tugged on the tall, tight collar of the blouse. "No wonder everyone thinks servants are so abused."

She pulled my hand down and straightened the collar. "Do not think me rude, Miriam, but perhaps I should speak on your behalf."

I raised an eyebrow. "Why?"

She chuckled. "Your manner of speaking is rather curt, and some might take offense at your straightforward speech."

I tugged on the collar again. "All right, but just remember we're going to the Sus Tavi."

Darda pulled my hand down again. "I remember. Now let's be off."

We climbed out of the hold and into the afternoon sun. The light glistened off the deep blue waters of the harbor and warmed the faces of the merchants and sailors. Darda led the way off the ship and through the crowds that bustled all over the docks.

This being only my second view of the city, I ogled the sights like a farm girl fresh from the countryside. The clean walls shimmered in the bright sun, and many had long flower beds with brightly colored plants. The alleys and wide roads were crowded with locals and people who took in the sights like I did. Most had plain-cloth clothes like those I wore, but the richer folks had fine silk attire and wide hats to keep their complexion pale.

We reached the square where Darda turned left to the part of the city that abutted the mountains. The broad boulevards narrowed and the houses, though still two floors, grew shorter and stockier. The whitewash grew older, and in some places was chipped and broken. There were fewer windows and even fewer flower pots.

The once straight streets meandered like a dragon toward the mountain. The walls of the houses grew so close I wondered if my shoulders would be too wide. A few scraggly-dressed people sat in the shallow doorways. Some of them looked up and scowled at us as we passed, but most ignored us.

I stayed so close to Darda I nearly became her shadow. "Are you sure you know where you're going?" I whispered as we passed a seedy looking restaurant in the open ground floor of a squat building.

She nodded. "Yes. The Sus Tavi is in the older part of the city."

A thin shadow stepped into our path and blocked our way. The shadow lifted their head and revealed himself to be a rough-looking customer with an unshaven face and a long smirk. The man's skin was a ghastly shade of green and his eyes were slits of yellow. His dark, beady eyes flickered between us, and he spoke in a voice so raspy it sounded like two pieces of sandpaper being rubbed together. "What are a pair of pretty girls like you wanting with the Sus Tavi when Ah've got a much better place fer ya to go."

Darda scowled at him. "We have no business with you, sir, and only wish to pass."

He stepped toward us. "But Ah'm making you my business."

I stepped back and bumped into something hard. I spun around and found myself staring up into a similar disheveled face, but this one had some piggish qualities. The sus grinned at me and widened his nostrils. "This one's pretty nice looking."

The first man glared at him. "Ah found 'em first so Ah get to choose which one Ah get."

His companion's grin grew wider. "Wha don't we take 'em to the Market? Women are always likin' to go to the Market."

The thin man laughed and slapped his leg. "That's the best idea ya ever had, mate! Ah'll get the skinny one and you can get the other one." The men raised their arms and stalked toward us.

"This skinny one says no," I retorted before I ducked his arms.

Darda turned and revealed her wings. They flew out and hit the sus in the face, but the thin one ducked. "Run, Miriam!" she yelled at me.

"Not without you!" I insisted.

She pushed me back the way we came. "Run and tell Magnus!"

I stumbled back past where the sus stood. He grunted and lunged at Darda, tackling her to the ground. The lithe man dove over them and landed on all fours in front of me. His long, slithery tongue flicked out. "Yer not going-" I spun around and fled.

I raced down the narrow street and risked a glimpse over my shoulder. The slithery man jumped from wall to wall criss-crossing the small road. He flew over my head and landed on two feet just a few feet in front of me. I slammed into his chest as he turned around. His wiry arms wrapped around me and pinned me to his bony chest.

"Yer a feisty one, ain't ya? We'll have to take care of that for a bit." He shoved his palm against my face. A scent like bitter almonds wafted into my nostrils. The world spun around me until I lost consciousness.

CHAPTER 6

"Miriam."

It was so dark, and the voice sounded so far away. All I wanted to do was go back to sleep.

"Miriam!"

I wrinkled my nose and tried to get comfortable, but I couldn't move my arms. Something chafed my wrists.

"SOLD!"

The booming voice startled me awake. My eyes flew open and were met with a terrifying world of scum and rank water. I was leaned against a slime-covered brick wall, and before me was a large man-made, or in this case probably dragon-made, cavern of sloped brick. The space was some hundred feet square and the ceiling reached forty feet above my head. The area was also packed to capacity, with wall-to-wall coverage of men and women. They stood in front of a platform some ten feet from me.

I wasn't the only one lined up on the wall. There were some dozen other women, including Darda close beside me. I shifted and found my wrists and ankles were bound by a thick rope.

I turned to Darda. "What the hell is going on-"

"Next up for the auction!" a man on the platform called. He wore a robe of bright yellow cloth and swept one of his long-sleeve arms over our lineup. "A beauty snatched from the horrors of the streets and set within this gem of a place." That got a laugh from the crowd. "I present to you for your delights, the Pale Beauty!"

A man in black garb with a hood over his head marched up to me and grabbed my bound wrists. He yanked me to my feet and dragged me up the short flight of stairs that led up to the top of the platform. The man stopped us in the center of the platform and faced me toward the crowd. Whoops, hollers and whistles arose from the crowd.

The auctioneer in the loud robes stepped up beside me and grinned. "I can see we have many interested customers. May I start the bidding at three drachma?"

"Three!" someone shouted.

"Five!" another called out.

"Five and an obol!" a man yelled. That got a laugh from the crowd.

The auctioneer smiled. "I see we have a very high bidder among us."

"Six drachma!"

"Seven!"

"Humble Hubert."

A hush fell over the crowd. My hooded captor stiffened.

The auctioneer's face turned a lovely shade of pasty white. He hurried to the edge of the platform and swept his eyes over the crowd. "Who said that? Well?"

A single arm raised in the crowd. My heart skipped a beat when I recognized Tillit. The crowd parted for him and the hog-nosed man strode forward to stand before the platform.

The auctioneer glared at him. "Is this a jest?"

Tillit shook his head. "Nope. I call Humble Hubert."

"B-but the auction! The drachma! My commission-"

"So you're going against it?" Tillit challenged him.

The auctioneer swallowed a lump in his throat and shook his head. "N-no, of course not-"

"And I need another one." Tillit nodded at Darda. "That one."

"Whatta ya mean taking our girls?" a man spoke up. The green-skinned fellow from before stepped out of the crowd and sneered at Tillit. "What's yer proof of Humble Hubert?"

Tillit drew out a small coin from his pocket and flipped it to the snake man. Our foe caught it in his hand and gazed down at his palm. His eyes widened so much I thought they were going to pop.

Tillit grinned and walked over to snatch the coin from the stupefied fellow. "Now if you don't mind, I'll be taking them."

He turned to the platform and looked past me at the hooded fellow. "Untie her ropes and the other one."

The man fumbled to obey, and soon Darda and I stood together near the wall. I looked up as Tillit came up to us.

"What's going-" He grasped my arm and pressed a finger to his lips.

"In a bit," he whispered. He shoved me to our left and down the wall behind the platform, and spoke in a louder voice so everyone could hear. "Come on now! Get a move on!"

Darda and I were herded by Tillit through a door in the wall and into a low, narrow tunnel made from the same brick. A steady trickle of water flowed down the center of the three-foot wide passage. The area was lit by torches placed some ten feet apart on the wall opposite the door.

Tillit slammed the wood door shut and jerked his head to his left. We followed him down the dark passage and around a corner where he stopped and turned to us. His eyes flickered from me to Darda and back to me. "Was it that scaly idiot who brought you two to the Market?"

Darda nodded. "Yes. He and another kidnapped us as we sought to reach the Sus Tavi."

He arched an eyebrow. "What were you going there for?"

"To see you," I spoke up.

He clucked his tongue and shook his head. "You almost saw the inside of a harem. And you-" he returned his attention to Darda, "-you should've known better than to be walking through the Tavi part of the city."

Darda straightened and pursed her lips. "The city has not improved since I was last along those streets."

He scoffed. "I'll say it hasn't. Not much is improving nowadays."

"Why?" I asked him.

He shook his head. "Never mind that. What were you wanting from me?"

"I wanted you to show me around," I told him.

Tillit arched an eyebrow, but the corners of his lips twitched upward. "The lady of the White Castle was wanting me to show her the city?"

"'White Castle?'" I repeated.

Tillit chuckled. "You do need someone to show you around, don't you? The White Castle is what Xander's humble home is called."

"He is Lord Xander," Darda scolded him.

Tillit shrugged. "Not down here, and I think he'd feel the same." He tapped the side of his nose. "It's best to keep your business, and your title, to yourself in these tunnels."

I looked around us. "What *are* these tunnels?"

Tillit rapped the brick wall with one of his knuckles. "The old cistern system for the city. They dug the tunnels a couple thousand years ago, but they haven't been used much since a new line was built by Xander's dad a couple centuries ago."

"And you knew that such illegal activity was harbored in these tunnels?" Darda questioned him.

Tillit pursed his lips. "You don't like it then you figure out how to fix it."

She frowned at him. "I certainly will. Our Lord will come down here and-"

"-make a mess of everything, and the rats'll scurry deeper into their holes where it'll be harder for me to follow 'em," Tillit finished. He leaned a shoulder against one of the damp walls and folded his arms. "You want so that I can't get anyone out of here? Cuz that would be the way to do it."

"So you would let them go at their dastardly business?" she countered.

"The world's always going to be filled with dastardly business. I just try to do my part to see it isn't too dastardly," he replied.

I raised my hand. "Could we have this conversation someplace that isn't so wet?" I lifted the damp hem of my dress and showed off my soaked shoes.

Tillit smiled and pushed off from the wall. "You wanted to go to the Sus Tavi, so I'll take you there."

CHAPTER 7

Tillit guided us through the maze of disused cistern tunnels and to a wooden ladder that led up a hole to a hatch. He grasped the rungs and grinned at us. "I'd say ladies first, but seeing as how we're short on them right now I'll take the lead."

I hid my smile and Darda glared at him. Tillit led the way up the rickety ladder and through the hatch. It brought us into a large storage room filled with small crates marked with animals of every variety and enough foreign languages to fill a peace conference. The crates were stacked nearly to the ceiling, but were lined up so there were halls between the large stacks so any box could be grabbed. All roads led to a thick wooden door through which was blasted a cacophony of loud laughter and clinking cups.

LABYRINTH OF THE DRAGON

Tillit stepped in front of us and turned so his back faced the door. He spread his arms out and smiled. "Welcome to Sus Tavi and the world's largest collection of drinks."

Darda wrinkled her nose. "We are not here for the liquor."

The sus grinned and slid up to a case. "That's too bad. I thought maybe you'd want some of this."

He slipped his hand beneath the lid and pulled out a clear glass bottle with a long neck. The contents were a strange purple color with bits of something floating inside.

Darda's eyes widened at the bottle before she narrowed them at the sus. "How do you know that?"

Tillit chuckled and tossed the bottle at her. She fumbled it for a few seconds before she pressed it against her chest. "I make it my business to know the weaknesses of my friends and my enemies. Anyway, let's go sit down and have ourselves a little drink." He walked up to us and winked. "After all, it's on the house."

Darda straightened like her feathers were ruffled. I hid my smile behind a cough as Tillit led us through the wood door and into the front part of the establishment. The Sus Tavi was a large bar with minimal light and even more minimal cleaning. A bar took up the back corner of the business, and on the wall behind the long bar were shelves of the bottles that were stored in the back room. Round wood tables, some propped up with empty crates, littered the room. The chairs, some of which *were* crates, were even more scattered and partially broken.

Men, if you could call them that, were huddled together. Sometimes small objects traded hands, sometimes it was just a piece of paper. They glanced over their shoulders like they expected a bust any minute.

Tillit led us over to an empty table in one of the darkest corners where we sat down. I looked around. "How come this one wasn't taken?"

He leaned back and grinned. "Let's just say this one's reserved."

I arched an eyebrow. "For people who know Humble Herbert?"

The conversations close to us stopped. The men looked over their shoulders and stared at us with dark eyes. I sheepishly smiled and waved at them. They sneered and turned their sullen faces away.

Tillit cleared his throat and leaned over the table toward me. He dropped his voice so low I could barely hear him over the constant hum over secretive chatter. "That's not really a name you're supposed to throw around in here, or anywhere else."

"So what does it mean, and what was on that coin you gave to that lizard?" I asked him.

He smiled. "Your first lesson of the day is the word 'gamme.'"

I blinked at him. "Come again?"

"That 'lizard' that took you, that's what he is. A gamme," Tillit told me.

"And that means what?" I persisted.

Tillit leaned back and hailed the bar with his finger. "It means you have a lot to learn about this world, and that he was a snake, not a lizard."

A young woman from the bar came over to us. She wore her dirty-blond hair in a tight bun and a dirty apron over her front. "What'll you have?"

"Three glasses, and a platter of meat," Tillit told her. She nodded and strolled away.

"Are all 'gamme' that friendly?" I asked him.

He grinned. "Most of them. For me I wouldn't put trust in one in a hundred of that species."

"Such horrible creatures. . ." Darda murmured.

Tillit chuckled as the woman brought back three glasses and a platter of meat. "Careful there, my dear. They're your cousin-in-laws, you know."

"Cousins?" I wondered.

Tillit took the bottle from Darda and popped the cork. "You don't think your world's the only one with evolution, do you?"

I arched an eyebrow. "What do you know about my world?"

He shrugged as he poured out three glasses of the purple stuff. A sweet scent of berries hit my nostrils. "Oh, whatever I can. I'd like to know more, of course, but first I have to repay you."

I blinked at him. "Me?"

He nodded as he pushed the glasses in front of us. "Yep. Without both of you I probably wouldn't have gotten out of there, at least not that easily." He raised his glass. "A toast to the hero of the forest."

I raised my glass and Darda reluctantly followed suit. We clinked glasses and I gingerly took a sip of the drink. The liquid had a full-body flavor of berries mixed with a hint of wine.

I looked to Darda. "Wow. I can see why you like this stuff."

"It's a fresh shipment from the hinterlands around Alexandria," Tillit commented. "A fine berry aged to perfection in wine barrels." He put down his empty glass and looked me over. "So what were you wanting from me exactly? The grand tour, or something a little more fun?"

A crooked smile slipped onto my lips. "What's in the fun?"

Darda spit some of her berry wine back in her glass and frowned at me. "Miriam."

Tillit laughed. "Don't worry too much. I can't get you into much more trouble than you already got yourself into. Besides-" he studied me with a peculiar glint in his eyes, "-I think our little hero here would enjoy this."

I shrugged. "Why not? When can we go?"

"Just as soon as I do some justice of my own on this stuff." He poured another glass and downed the whole thing before he took a handful of food and stuffed it into his mouth.

Darda shrank back from his piggish way of eating. "Haven't you learned any manners in these fifty years?"

Tillit paused and tilted his head to one side in thought. Then he shook his head. "Nope." And indulged in more piggish behavior.

I furrowed my brow and pointed my finger between them. "You two know each other?"

Darda pursed her lips as she watched the horrible sight before us. "Yes, for a brief time."

Tillit laughed between bites. "You were prudish then. I thought maybe you being around Cate would have mellowed you out a little."

"Don't speak of her so lightly," Darda snapped.

I looked from one to the other. "Who's Cate?"

A shadow passed over Darda's face, and even Tillit paused in his eating to look up at me. His eyes flickered to the servant. "Does she know anything?"

Darda cleared her throat. "She knows what she must."

Tillit frowned. "Then not much."

My heart skipped a couple of beats. "What don't I know?" I asked them.

Darda looked Tillit in the eyes. "It was you who brought up the subject, but I wish to explain to her what I can."

He scoffed. "Which isn't as much as she should know."

"What don't I know?" I spoke in a voice loud enough to echo over the room. This time I got the attention of all of those present in the Tavi. The ugly mugs looked over their shoulders and glared at our table.

Tillit set down his glass for the last time beside the empty bottle of berry alcohol and stood. "I think it's time we took a walk."

CHAPTER 8

Darda and I didn't argue. Tillit tossed down some coins and led us out the more stylish front door. The Tavi sat on one of the old narrow streets just one block away from the base of the steep, rocky mountain range. Nearby was a small square that abutted one of the steeple-topped churches I'd seen on my way into the city. The whitewash was faded, but the wood siding was sturdy and a glass window above the pair of doors signified a healthy service. Atop the window was another of those sword symbols.

One of the doors opened. A young woman with a tiny daughter at her side stepped out. With them was a man in a cloak of such a dark blue hue it was almost black. He smiled and bowed his head to them. "May you find peace as calm as the waters, my daughter."

LABYRINTH OF THE DRAGON

She returned the bow, and I saw a necklace with the sword pendant hung around her neck. The same for her young daughter. "Thank you, Father, and the same to you." The three parted company. The man stepped back into the building and shut the door.

I nodded at the building. "Is that some sort of church?"

Darda nodded. "It is. The worshipers pay homage to the lord of the lake, and in return he is said to grant them protection from disaster."

"That guy's gotta have a busy calendar with all those people making their pleas to him," Tillit quipped as he strolled down the street.

I hurried after him and Darda followed. "Don't think I've forgotten that you're not telling me something I'm supposed to know."

Darda hurried up behind us, but couldn't squeeze in because of the narrow street. "My Lady-"

"Miriam," I reminded her.

"Miriam, there is no need to be concerned about the past," she assured me.

"That's something I'd like to decide for myself," I returned.

Tillit chuckled. "You remind me a lot of Cate. She had your spirit, and stubbornness."

"So what happened to her?" I asked them.

Tillit's face fell and he tilted his head up to look at the darkening sky. Night would soon be upon us. "She died. It was fifty years ago that it happened."

"I requested that I be the one to tell her, Mr. Tillit," Darda reminded him.

He shrugged. "Suit yourself."

Darda cleared her throat and sidled up to me as we entered the small square. A round well with a gable roof sat in the center of the area. "My Lord's mother was a very kind woman. She cared very deeply for the people of Alexandria and in turn they loved her-"

"Stop making her sound like a saint. She had too much spirit for that," Tillit scolded her.

She glared at him. "She was a very good person."

Tillit stopped us twenty feet from the door of the church and gestured to the building. "Did she ever go to church?"

Darda straightened and turned her nose up. "No, but-"

"Did she *not* drink berry wine?"

"She did, but-"

"And didn't she sneak out of the castle every once in a while to have some fun with her Tillit?" he continued.

Darda put her foot down. "Mr. Tillit, I was aware of her doings, but-"

"But nothing. That woman was real, more than any of us, and she didn't deserve what happened to her," he snapped.

My heart dropped into my stomach and my voice was half its strength. "What happened to her?"

Darda's face fell. "Cate was killed in the castle by an intruder."

"That's keeping the story clean," Tillit quipped.

Her eyes flickered to him. "I do not wish to worry the young lady."

My face must have resembled a sheet. "Worry me about what?"

"About the raids going on and what happened at the Portal," Tillit commented.

I blinked at him. "What about them?"

"Because they were done by the same people who murdered her," he told me.

"Mr. Tillit, that is quite enough!" Darda growled. She looped her arms around one of mine and glared at him. "Can you not see how frightened she is?"

He shrugged. "She's got to know the truth some time."

"Now is not that time, not when she has so much on her mind," she argued.

Tillit studied my pale face for a moment before a crooked grin slipped onto his pudgy lips. "Nah, she'll take it. Like I said, she's got spirit. That's why I want to show her something."

"It had better not be dangerous," Darda warned him.

He shook his head. "Nope. You might even like it, Darda."

Her feathers were ruffled again. "I will not have you be so familiar with me."

He held up his hands. "All right, all right, I won't call you anything I would say in polite company. Seeing as we're not in polite company, however-"

"Mr. Tillit," she growled.

He laughed. "Fine, I'll be good." He looked down at me half-embraced in Darda's arms and caught my eyes. "So you want to see it, or do you want to go back to that castle and Renner?"

With those choices I stood straight and swallowed the lump in my throat. "I'll stay out here."

Tillit slipped to my side and slapped me on the back. "What spirit! Now let's be off. It's just a few blocks this way."

I didn't want to admit it, but the reveal about Xander's mom left me with a shiver that ran up and down my spine in an endless loop of fear. Darda stuck close to me and eyed every stranger like they were a prospective assassin.

The quiet between us was maddening, so I leaned toward Tillit in front of us to catch his attention. "So where are we going exactly?"

"To the lake," he told me.

"What have you to show us there?" Darda questioned him.

He looked over his shoulder and grinned at us. "You'll see."

I looked around at the old buildings and streets. "So how old is this city, anyway?"

"The earliest parts of the city are over seven thousand years old," Darda told me.

"That's some history," I commented. I glanced up at the towering mountain to our right. "Has it ever been taken?"

She pursed her lips and looked ahead. "Yes, though the lords of the city have never lost control for very long."

"Get ready, my ladies. We're nearly there," Tillit announced.

We reached the end of the street and stepped out into the wide expanse that overlooked the lake. Our view of the clear, calm waters wasn't quite unbroken. Before us was the small strip of land that connected the shoreline to the small island of the lake god. The peak of the obelisk shimmered in the last light of the day. The narrow gravel path that led to the shrine was dotted with short lamps, but they weren't lit.

That was about to change. A short figure hopped from the direction of the shrine toward us. In their hand was a small stick with a lit end like those used to light fireworks. The figure stopped at each of the lamps and lit them. The person paused some ten feet from us and lit the last of the lamps.

The illumination gave me a good look at their stooped figure. The most pronounced part of the man's three-foot body was their humped back. The lump forced them to stoop until their thick front arms and hands nearly dragged the ground. Their long brown hair stretched down their back and peeked between their bent knees. The man lifted his head and stared at us with a pair of bright blues eyes.

Tillit opened his arms and walked toward the man. "Good evening, Kumar!"

The stooped man sneered at him. His voice was deep and had a melodious sound to it. "What do you want?"

Tillit swept his arm over the island and inlet. "We just want a look around these lovely grounds you take such good care of."

"Then look and leave me alone," Kumar snapped. He turned and hopped back in the direction he came.

Darda and I caught up to Tillit, and I nodded at the retreating figure. "Is he another species in this world?"

Tillit looked over his shoulder and showed a mischievous grin on his lips. "You don't recognize your own kind?"

"So he's human?" I guessed.

He turned to face us and shook his head. "No, at least not completely." He jerked his head at Kumar's back. "That's what happens when a fae breeds with a human, and things don't turn out so well."

I cringed. "How horrible."

Tillit winked at me. "Makes you feel lucky, doesn't it?"

I stared blankly at him. "Come again?"

He clicked his tongue and shook his head. "Come come, my dear Neito Vedesta, you can't hide something that important from old Tillit."

"You mustn't speak so in the open," Darda scolded him.

He held up his hands. "All right, calm down. I'll be good, but-" his eyes flickered to me, "-I'm going to find you out. You just wait and see."

My face fell. "I wish you'd find us a nice place to sit. My feet are killing me."

Tillit laughed and walked backwards with his customary bag bouncing against his hip. "I think I can arrange that."

CHAPTER 9

Tillit led us down the lit path and onto the small island. Evenly-spaced trees lined the shore, but the front that looked out on the lake was left open to a breathtaking view of the waters and the castle. The high mountains that encircled the lake were like tall sentinels that guarded the city and its majestic seat of governance.

A long bench with a backing stretched across the grassy ground and sat just above the lapping water. I sat on the bench and looked out on the scenery. A soothing breeze washed over me and stirred my hair.

Tillit came up and stood beside me. His eyes, too, focused on the grand view before us. "Nice and peaceful, isn't it?"

I smiled and nodded. "Very." I looked up at him. "Thank you for bringing us here."

He turned his face away from me and shrugged. "It was nothing. You were going to see it some time, anyway."

I glanced over my shoulder at the towering obelisk with its small shrine. A portico with thick, intricately-topped columns was attached to the front of the short building, and the double-doors were open to the interior. Torches lit the inside, and a statue glistened in the flickering light. I frowned and stood.

"Miriam?" Darda asked me as she grasped my arm. "Is something wrong?"

I nodded at the statue. "What's that?"

Tillit followed my gaze and smiled. "Let's go and see."

We walked across the grassy ground and followed the gravel walk that looped up to the portico. Stepping into the small shrine was like entering a different world. The air was heavy with incense and an echo of chants long since spoken. With each flicker of the torches the darkness marched forward and retreated into the far corners, seemingly reaching for and drawing back from visitors. Above us was the pitched ceiling with its stone roof that tightly sealed the large, single room.

Along the walls were shelves upon shelves of small offerings. There were tiny statues of buildings, carved figures of people, and even some wooden coins.

The centerpiece of the room, however, was the statue that sat in the center and rear of the space. The statue was carved from a single block of white rock of the surrounding mountains. The figure was a tall, naked man who stood among a spray of waves. He looked to be about forty, and sported a long beard. His long hair draped over his shoulders and spread down to his thighs. The figure was so real that the eyes seemed to stare back at me.

LABYRINTH OF THE DRAGON

I nodded at the statue and couldn't force my voice above a whisper. "Who's that?"

"That is Beriadan, ruler of the lake of the same name and a mighty powerful fae," Tillit told me.

I stepped forward and squinted as I studied the face. "He looks a lot like the fae guy I saw in the river."

"That's not surprising. All Mare fae are related," Tillit admitted.

Darda moved to stand beside me and looked into my face. "Are you feeling well, Miriam? Perhaps this has been too much for you."

"Don't treat the girl like she's a baby!" Tillit scolded her as he moved to my other side. "She can take care of herself."

Darda leaned forward to glare across my front at Tillit. "We have been out long enough. We should return to the castle."

Tillit frowned. "You've barely seen anything!"

"We've seen quite enough," she argued.

Their jabbering voices receded into the background as I continued to stare at those white eyes. One of the hands of the statue was held out as though to take it. I reached for it and set my hand gingerly atop the cold stone. A shiver shot through me. I drew my hand back, but hesitated on the outstretched fingers. I put pressure on them.

One of the fingers drew down. I heard a faint click and the floor behind the statue slid away to reveal a winding staircase that disappeared into darkness.

Darda grabbed my shoulders and drew me back. "What is this? What's going on?"

Tillit eyed me with a keen look. "How'd you know that was there, My Lady?"

I shook my head. "I don't know. I just knew I needed to set my hand there."

"What is this about?" Darda questioned us both. She nodded at the hole. "What is that doing here?"

A twinkle slipped into Tillit's eyes as he walked around the statue and stepped into the hole. "Come on down and I'll show you," he dared.

He walked down the stairs and out of sight. I made to follow him, but Darda held me back. "We cannot go down there!"

I frowned at her. "Why not?"

"There might be more of those ruffians like beneath the city!" she pointed out.

I smiled and patted her hand. "Tillit's with us. I'm sure we'll be fine." Besides, I had a tugging feeling that demanded I go down there. "Now let's go."

Darda reluctantly followed me around the statue and down the winding stairs. I heard a soft tap above me and looked up. The hatch had shut. My heart skipped a couple of beats.

"It's all right! The hatch can open from this side!" Tillit called to us.

I swallowed and continued down. A faint blue light guided us to the bottom of the steps and into a wondrous world. A long passage stretched in either direction from the end of the island and into the city. The hall was lit by the very walls itself. They were made of a smooth blue crystal that pulsed with a soft blue light. The crystal was so transparent I could see through it to the waters around the island. Fish swam a few yards from us and water weeds swayed back and forth against the current.

LABYRINTH OF THE DRAGON

I pressed my hand against the crystal and felt a strange warmth. I looked to Tillit who stood nearby. "What is this place?"

He spread his arms and turned in a circle. "This is the Labyrinth of Alexandria."

Darda's eyes widened. "The Labyrinth? Surely you jest."

Tillit smiled and shook his head. "It's no joke. It's as real as you or I, unless we're merely a figment of someone's imagination."

"What about this labyrinth?" I asked them.

Tillit gestured to Darda. "This time I will let the lady speak."

Darda cleared her throat. "The Labyrinth was-"

"Is," Tillit corrected her.

She glared at him, but continued. "The Labyrinth *was* rumored to be an ancient system of tunnels beneath the city of Alexandria. The ancient ancestors of the dragons built them to protect themselves from men."

"Why didn't they just fly away?" I wondered.

Tillit tapped the illuminated ground beneath our feet with his toes. "Because when your enemy knows you can fly they won't expect you to be in the ground."

Darda frowned. "You gave me the floor, Mr. Tillit."

He smiled and bowed to her. "I did, and I give it back to you."

Darda returned her attention to me. "The tunnels were carved from a blue rock that was said to shine in the darkest of nights and be as strong as the best of steel."

Tillit rapped his knuckle against the wall. There was a hollow sound to it, and a little bit of the rock crumbled to the ground. "I think we can scratch that one off as myth."

Darda gave him a warning glare and continued. "After the fall of men the Labyrinth was closed and lost to history."

Tillit folded his arms over his chest and shook his head. "That's not quite how the story goes."

She glared at him. "Then how does the tale end, Mr. Tillit?"

He swept his eyes over the passage. "These tunnels were found by *my* ancestors when we dug the shrine. We've been using them ever since."

Darda set her hands on her hips. "And you never told Lord Xander?"

He shrugged. "Didn't seem worth the trouble. Besides, not that many know about them now, and most of them would like to keep it hush-hush, if you know what I mean."

"I do not know what you mean," she snapped.

He smiled and jerked his head down the passage that led toward the city. "Then I'll show you."

Tillit led us down the passage some fifty feet. The floor declined so we dropped another ten feet before the way opened into a huge cavern. The walls were the same brilliant, glowing blue color, and a sparkling dome topped the area. Six hallways opposite our own led off in different directions like a fan.

The room had round niches in the walls that were half a foot tall and just as wide. They started a foot from the floor and rose up thirty feet which fell short of the forty-foot ceiling.

I approached a niche and saw it held a small bottle covered in a thin layer of gold plating. A small plaque wrapped around the front half of the base. I picked it up and peered at the writing. It was Latin, but I wasn't that familiar with that tongue.

LABYRINTH OF THE DRAGON

"You might want to put that down," Tillit called from the entrance.

I looked to him. "Why?"

"Because whoever's ashes those are won't appreciate being dropped."

I felt the color drain from my face. "Ashes?"

He grinned. "Yep. You're holding a dead person there."

I stuffed the urn back in its niche and stepped back. A quick look around told me there were hundreds of similar urns in the thousands of niches. "Who are they?"

"You mean who were they," he corrected me as he strolled over to a spot along the wall close to me. He pulled an urn from a niche and lifted it up to admire the workmanship. "The plaques on the bottom tell their story. This one here was a rich merchant some eight hundred years ago. He owned a hundred ships and traded throughout the world." He set the person back and plucked another one from the wall. "This young lady here took over her father's business and doubled the wealth that she left to her young son."

"But why are they here?" I persisted.

"They're the elite of the sus history," he told me as he set the urn back. He nodded at the walls. "This is a vault of the wealthiest sus in the world, at least when they were alive. They all became wealthy because of the docks of Alexandria and decided to have their remains interred here to be close to the lake deity who they believed blessed them with their wealth."

"Sus buried in the Labyrinth?" Darda gasped.

He grinned. "Yep, but don't be to put-out. It's only the wealthiest who get put down here."

I furrowed my brow. "But isn't the person in the lake just a fae? You make him sound like a god."

"Would you have considered King Thorontur on par with the other fae?" he asked me.

I shrugged. "I guess not, but I still wouldn't say he was a god."

"Some of these fae are pretty old, and all those years stack up to a lot of knowledge and power," he pointed out. He nodded at the blue walls around us. "Beriadan's one of those fellows. He's been around a lot longer than the dragons and humans, and he'll be around a lot-" He paused and half-turned to one of the passages close to us. His eyebrows crashed down. "That's funny."

"I very much doubt it," Darda quipped.

Tillit pressed his finger to his lips. He held very still as his nostrils pushed in and out. His eyes widened and he spun around to grab me. "Come on!"

The sus shoved me toward the wall to the right of our passage and took Darda along for the ride. He shoved us near the urns and pressed down on the top of one. The wall proved to be a false painting and opened to reveal a hidden space barely large enough to fit two people. Tillit pushed us into the secret wall and pressed on the urn, shutting us in.

And just in time.

CHAPTER 10

Though there was a painting in front of us, the blue walls around us gave us light with which to see each other. Darda pounded her fist on the wall. "Let us out!"

"Shut up," Tillit hissed.

A marching noise rang through the cavern. There were numerous eye holes in the painting that looked out past the urns at the cavern. Darda and I held our breaths and looked through the holes.

A group of six sus and one man marched out of the second passage on the left. The leader of the group, a man with an ugly scar that stretched from his temple down to his chin, wore a suit of cloth clothes devoid of any speck of dust. The others under his charge, however, were covered from head-to-toe in filthy so thick only a pig would have been happy to see them. Some of the sus looked pretty happy, themselves. That is, until they saw Tillit beside the our wall. Their gleeful expressions fell off their faces and turned to nasty snarls.

Tillit held up his hands as they slowly circled three sides of him. "Good evening, gentlemen. Nice night for a walk, isn't it?"

The clean one stepped to the forefront and looked Tillit over. "What are you doing here?"

Tillit nodded at the urns. "Just admiring some dead people."

The leader's eyes flickered to one of the larger sus who stepped toward Tillit. "You chose a bad night to admire them."

The sus lunged for Tillit with his arms wide open. Our sus looked down at his feet and frowned. "What's that?" He ducked just as the man reached him so his arms wrapped around nothing. Tillit stood straight and his head knocked into the jaw of his would-be attacker. There was a hard crack and the man yelped before he stumbled back clutching his jaw.

Tillit blinked at the man. "What happened to you?"

"Grab him," the leader ordered his men.

The five other sus jumped Tillit. He pulled off his bag off his shoulder and draped the strap over the first two before he gave a twist and tied them together. They knocked heads and sunk to the floor. Another sus grabbed him from behind, but Tillit pushed off the floor and slammed him into the rear wall close beside the fake one. That one slumped to the floor. The other two were quickly dispatched with some nice dodging and quick uppercuts.

LABYRINTH OF THE DRAGON

Tillit turned to the center of the room and froze. The man had his dragon clawed fingers pressed against Tillit's throat. He'd moved without anyone seeing him.

"I'll ask you again, who are you?" the dragon demanded to know.

Tillit's eyes flickered down to the man's red-clawed hand. "The edict said you weren't supposed to come back here."

The dragon sneered and slammed his fist into Tillit's temple. Our friend crumpled to the floor to lay beside so many of his defeated.

The man stepped back and reverted his hand back to the human form. "Get up!" he snapped. The sus struggled to their feet and cradled their injuries. He nodded at Tillit. "Pick him up."

One of them tossed Tillit roughly over their shoulder and the group disappeared down the same hallway they'd come.

I waited until I was sure they were gone and then I pressed my hands against the wall and pushed. Nothing happened. "We have to get out of here!" I told Darda.

"Perhaps there is a switch," she suggested.

She and I looked around for something out the ordinary. My eyes fell on a knob of crystal above and in front of her head. "There! Press that!"

Darda slammed her palm against the knob. The rock sunk into the fake wall, and the whole thing swung open. I rushed out first and snatched up Tillit's bag. The strap was torn in two. I grasped the bag and looked in the direction they'd gone.

Darda grabbed my arm and tugged me toward the hallway from which we came. "Quickly! We must hurry!"

I yanked my arm free of her grasp and glared at her. "I may not know much about this world, but I know when someone's in trouble, and right now that someone is Tillit."

"We must inform Lord Renner of what happened. He will know what course of action to take," she suggested.

I took a step toward the hallway down which they had disappeared. "Then you go tell Renner and I'll go find Tillit."

Darda stood straight and lifted her chin. "I have never left my lady behind, and I will not start now."

I grabbed her hand and pulled her "Then you're coming with me, and no unnecessary noises."

"But Miriam-"

"That's unnecessary."

We hurried down the long, twisting passage after our friend and foes. They had a head-start, and we had no idea what dangers lurked ahead. Another problem presented itself, or rather four problems, when we reached an intersection and found ourselves staring at four diverging paths. I looked from one to the others, but there was no sign or sound of anyone.

"Damn it. . ." I muttered.

"Perhaps we should-" I rushed off into the second from the left hoping they had been consistent. "Miriam! Wait"

I knew it was stupid of me. This was a labyrinth, after all, and for all I knew there were legends of booby-traps and false halls that led to dead-ends, possibly literally. My only excuse was I was desperate to save the funny sus I now called friend. Whatever they planned for him he didn't deserve it. Probably.

I was thinking all these thoughts and not thinking of where I was going. The floor started a steep decline that caught me off-guard. I stumbled forward as my legs picked up acceleration without my permission. The passage became steeper and steeper and I got faster and faster. I slipped onto my butt in hopes of stopping my momentum, but my rear slid on the smooth blue rock.

"Miriam!" Darda called.

I twisted around and saw her hand outstretched toward me. Her other one was transformed into a claw and hovered close to the left wall. Our palms slapped together and Darda slammed her transformed hand into the wall. Claw met crumbly rock. We slowed and stopped.

I breathed a sigh of relief. "Remind me never to go on a water slide again."

Darda smiled, but a chink beside her caught both our attentions. The rock in which her fingers were embedded broke away. We screamed as we slipped down the passage. Darda and I bounced off the hard walls and spun in circles.

Just when I thought I would lose my lunch I crashed face-first into a hard, flat floor. Tillit's bag made a nice cushion for my legs. Darda toppled onto me and knocked the wind from my lungs. I was still gasping for air when I felt a tremble in the floor.

I looked ahead and found myself staring at the toes of a black boot. My eyes wandered up a clothed body to the face of an amused sus woman. Behind her in the small cavern in which we found ourselves were a dozen other sus, but only men.

The woman jerked her head toward us. Two of her minions walked around her and grabbed our collars. They hoisted us to our feet and released us before stepping back.

Their leader folded her arms over her chest and grinned. "Well, well, what do we have here? A couple of mice in the cat's lair? Don't you know you're not allowed down here, little mice?"

Darda stepped forward, but I stuck out my arm to stop her. "The Labyrinth was built by dragons," she reminded them.

The woman looked over her shoulder at those behind her. "What do you think of that, men? The Labyrinth was built by dragons." A jeering laugh arose from her men. She returned her attention to us. "I hope you mice have a good reason for being down here because we cats don't care for company."

"Probably better than yours," I snapped.

The leader chuckled. "You're a brave mouse, and you've got a funny look in your eyes. What's your name, mouse?"

"You tell me yours first and I might think about it," I returned.

She leaned toward us with her hands on his hips and slipped a nice, big grin onto her fat lips. "The name is Humble Herbert, and you're in a mess of trouble."

CHAPTER 11

I stared at her with blinking eyes. "Seriously? You're Herbert?"

The woman laughed at me. "What were you expecting? A human man?"

I shrugged. "I don't know. I guess I was expecting a man, at least."

Herbert looked from me to Darda. "What are you two doing down here, anyway? And how'd you know about-" Her gaze fell on Tillit's bag behind us. She flickered her eyes back to me and narrowed them. "Where did you get that bag?"

"We found it in these caverns," I told her.

Her jaw stiffened. "You're lying. What happened to the owner of that bag?"

I pursed my lips. "He was kidnapped by a bunch of sus and a dragon."

Herbert's eyes widened. "Tillit? Kidnapped?"

I arched an eyebrow. "So he really does know you?"

Herbert pushed past me and picked up the bag. She studied the straps and turned the bag over in her hands. "Of course he knows me. He throws my name around enough to be my husband." She turned back to us. "Where did they take him?"

I shook my head. "I don't know. We were trying to follow where they went in these caves, but we took the wrong path and ended up down here."

The woman looked past us at her people and lifted the bag. "Search the caverns. Find him."

They hurried forward and each in turn sniffed the bag before they rushed off. In a few moments Darda and I were left alone with Herbert and the bag.

She strode past us toward one of the half dozen passages that littered the small cavern. "Come with me or I'll kill you where you stand."

With that kind of invitation who were we to refuse? Darda and I followed her down the tunnel and into a large maze of passages that twisted and turned. I was lost long before the blue walls were replaced with regular, non-transparent stone. We arrived at a wood door and Herbert marched inside.

Darda and I peeked into the room. It was a small chamber with a table, chairs, piles of gold and jewels in one corner, and a plank bed in another one. The bed was fascinating, but I had eyes only for the shiny things in the corner.

Herbert tossed the bag into one of the chairs and stood in front of the table. The top was covered in maps young and old. She studied them for a second before she tossed them aside, and repeated this for a half dozen maps until she stopped at one particularly large one.

"Where did you-" Herbert glanced over her shoulder and saw we stood in the doorway. She rolled her eyes and jerked her head toward the table. "Get in here and show me where they went, or I really will make good on that promise to kill you."

Darda and I joined her at the table. The map showed the main cavern close to the shrine along with its connecting passages. Those passages went off in all directions and covered the city like a spider web. Some met caverns large or small, others were dead-ends. A lot of strange symbols, like hollow circles or squiggly lines, dotted the map where the passages ended.

Darda pointed at the cavern and followed their path with her finger. "They went into this passage, but disappeared somewhere beyond the next cavern.

Herbert glanced between us. "What were you doing down here with him? Did any of you recognize his attackers?"

"They were not familiar to either of us," Darda told her.

Herbert looked to me. "Is she speaking for you, as well?"

I nodded. "Yeah."

She arched an eyebrow. "You don't speak like a typical human. Where are you from?" She glanced at Darda. "Both of you."

Darda straightened and pursed her lips. "That is none of your-"

"We're from the castle," I spoke up.

Herbert returned her attention to me while Darda frowned. "Why did Tillit show you the Labyrinth?"

"I'm new here and I asked him to show us around," I explained.

She narrowed her eyes at me. "So why didn't his kidnappers take you, too?"

"Because he hid us behind a wall that was too small to fit everyone," I told her.

Herbert closed her eyes and shook her head, but a ghost of a smile lay at the corners of her lips. "That fool. Always trying to shove someone out of the way of some speeding carriage." She opened her eyes and stiffened her jaw before she returned her attention to Darda. "I'm guessing you've been around here for a while. Was there anything special about any of these sus or the dragon? Anything they wore?"

Darda clasped her hands together in front of her and straightened. "I saw nothing I haven't seen before."

Herbert's eyes narrowed. "That's a slimy answer. What aren't you telling me?"

Darda's eyebrows crashed down. "Nothing that concerns you."

"Tillit said something about how the dragon wasn't supposed to come into the city," I spoke up.

"My Lady!" Darda scolded me.

I glared back at her and gestured to Herbert. "Can't you see this is going to be the fastest way to rescue Tillit, *if* he's still alive?"

Herbert turned around to face us and leaned her back against the table. "All right, 'fess up, you two. Who are you really? Nobody from the castle calls anybody by that title without them being someone important."

LABYRINTH OF THE DRAGON

Darda frowned. "That is-"

"-my business now," Herbert finished for her. "Now out with it."

Darda crossed her arms over her chest and scowled at the sus woman. "Who are you to order us about? A scoundrel? A thief?"

Herbert grinned and bowed her head. "Both, but you can stop with the flatteries."

"Do you expect us to place our faith in the hands of such a person as yourself?" Darda challenged her.

Our hostess's eyebrows shot down and she frowned. "Whatever your position in the castle is, in this place-" she gestured to the stone walls around us, "-you're lower than dirt. You couldn't even protect yourself when trouble came your way. You had to have Tillit do it for you. Now are you going to get off your high-horse and help me find him, or are we going to keep wasting time with me prying information out of you and have him wind up dead for helping you?"

"I expect you to release us at once," Darda insisted.

Herbert snorted. "If I release you it would be in the middle of this maze."

I hopped between them and held up my hands. "Ladies! Ladies! We're missing one sus, remember? And this isn't going to-" A tremor rattled the walls and floor. The shaking and rumbling grew worse with each successive second.

Herbert grabbed the table to keep herself from falling and whipped her eyes up to the ceiling. "What the hell?"

"An earthquake!" I shouted.

"This way!" Herbert ordered us as she grabbed up all the maps and raced for the door. Darda and I were so close on her heels we could have moonlighted as her boots. Our feet pounded the cold stone before we rushed into the blue light. We ran into a another sus at one of the intersections.

"A cave in the eastern block has fallen!" he told us.

"Then tell anyone you see to head west!" she snapped.

He nodded and rushed into a southern passage. Herbert led us down a path to our left.

"This way heads eastward!" Darda shouted.

"I need to find out what's causing this ruckus, and you're coming with me!" Herbert snapped.

Darda pursed her lips, and I wasn't too happy with this death-or-death scenario. The blue-lit corridors reached only a hundred yards away from the lake and was replaced by the hard stone of the mountains and plains. Torches lit our way, but half of them were snuffed out by debris.

After what felt like a thousand years and a million miles of running we reached the far eastern point of the city. The tremors only got worse and the cracking rocks fell like a sharp rain from the ceiling. I slipped on some of the coarse pebbles and knocked my shoulder into the wall. The hard, gray rock cut through my sleeve and jabbed into my flesh.

I cried out and clutched my shoulder as a thick stream of blood flowed from the wound. Herbert and Darda stopped.

"My Lady!" Darda yelled as she rushed to my side.

A loud noise above our heads made us pause and look up. A large crack appeared over our heads.

"Hit the wall!" Herbert shouted.

Darda slid up to me and pulled me to the ground against the wall. She covered me with her body as large rocks broke from the ceiling and rained down on us. The torches were extinguished and all light left the world. I felt something hard hit my head, and then I knew nothing.

CHAPTER 12

I was awoken by a soft scratching sound. *Great* I thought. *I'm going to be eaten by rats down here. I wonder if they even have rats in this world.*

The scratching sound was replaced by the loud scuff of rock against rock. I even heard the occasional grunt. Dust fell on my face and made me sneeze. The sounds stopped.

"Did you hear that?" someone spoke up.

"Keep digging!" a voice shouted.

The noises grew louder and more frantic. Rocks were hefted, and after a few minutes there was silence again. The soft light of a lantern shown across my face.

"My Lady!"

I forced my eyes open and found myself staring into the concerned face of Kinos, leader of the defense guards. Perched on his shoulder was his trusty hawk. He hovered over a small hole in the collapsed ceiling. Behind him was the bearded face of Magnus.

"How did you come to be down here?" he asked me.

I coughed on some dust in my dry throat. "Could I answer that someplace else?" I croaked.

Something shifted against me. I looked down and saw it was Darda. She still half-covered me, but a large boulder had knocked her off and trapped her beneath its hefty weight.

I grabbed her shoulders. "Oh my god! Darda? Darda, answer me!"

She raised her head and wearily smiled at me. "There is. . .no cause. . .for alarm. . .My Lady."

"Like hell there isn't," I retorted as I looked down at her trapped body.

"A moment and we will free you both!" Kinos promised.

I looked ahead of us at the collapsed tunnel. There was no sign of Herbert. "There's somebody else down here, too!" I shouted back. "A sus woman!"

"We will continue to look for her, but you must be freed first," Kinos insisted.

The men at his disposal were half-transformed dragon guards. They raised hundred-ton boulders like they were ten-pound weights and tossed them aside. In a few minutes Darda and I were dragged from our rocky prison and out into the darkness of late night.

The eastern portion of the beautiful city of Alexandria was changed. Some of the steeples leaned to one side, and many stone buildings had long cracks up their walls. The glow of fires lit up the dark sky and people called out for supplies or loved ones. The large gate was cracked and the walls were missing some chunks of stone. The few undamaged buildings were those that held the crest of the sword above their doorways. A steady stream of the robed fellows poured from the churches and assisted the frightened and wounded.

Darda and I were set on a wool blanket. Kinos knelt in front of us with Magnus behind him, and they both looked over our wounds.

After his quick perusal Kinos leaned back and smiled. "You were very fortunate. There are no broken bones, but your friend may need a long rest."

"Mere broken bones are worth saving My Lady," Darda replied.

Kinos pulled out a paper and pencil, and scribbled a note. He placed the note inside a tube attached to the hawk's leg and held out his arm. The hawk fluttered to his hand. "Castle." He tossed the hawk into the air and the bird flew off into the night. He returned his attention to us. "I must beg you now to satisfy my curiosity, My Lady. How did you come to be under such rubble?"

I nodded at the remains of the tunnel. "Could we find my friend first?"

He smiled. "Of course. I am sure they will be found in a few minutes."

I looked past him at the cave-in. The men had resumed their work looking for Herbert. They found her a few minutes later, unconscious but breathing. She was laid out beside us. Magnus and Kinos looked at her face and cast furtive glances at each other.

My heart quickened. "What? What is it?"

Kinos looked to me and shook his head. "There is nothing to fear, but how did you come to be in the company of this woman?"

I cringed. "You want the long or short of it?"

"The long, if you feel you have the strength."

I took a deep breath and recounted the events of the night. By the time we were finished Kinos had an astonished look on his face.

For his part, Magnus chuckled. "Quite a tale ya have there, My Lady. Fit for any sailor."

I rubbed my aching head and managed a grimacing smile. "I wish I'd only heard it and not lived it." A thought made me furrow my brow and look between the men. "But how'd you find us?"

Magnus grinned and tapped his eye patch. "Yer still carrying that soul stone around with ya, so it was easy to find such a thing among plain rock."

A familiar screech echoed above us and Kinos' hawk came into view. Kinos raised his arm and the bird landed. A note was rolled inside the tube.

Kinos removed the note and perused the contents. "It appears that Lord Renner will soon be joining us here to retrieve our Lady."

Magnus sneered and stood. "Then Ah'll be getting to helping somebody else." He tipped his head to me and smiled. "Mighty glad yer okay, My Lady, and you as well, Darda." Darda weakly smiled in return, and the captain limped off.

I turned my attention to my companions and nodded to the unconscious Herbert. "Will she be okay?"

Kinos followed my gaze and pursed his lips. "Yes, but sus are not so quick to heal as dragons or Maidens." His eyes flickered to me and studied my face. "Do you know who she is?"

I frowned. "I told you, she's Humble Herbert."

"But do you know what that name entails?"

I opened my mouth to reply, but the sound of galloping horses caught our attention. Our group turned toward the castle and watched a group of six horsemen with two empty-saddles steeds stampede down the street toward us. They reined in the horses ten feet from where we lay, and my heart sank as I recognized the lead as Renner.

He hopped down from the saddle and rushed over to me. "My Lady! Thank goodness you are safe!"

"Thanks to Darda," I added as I nodded to my weak friend.

Renner knelt in front of me and clasped one of my hands in both of his. "The gods must also be thanked for your safe return to us, but come. We must hurry you back to the castle before another quake occurs."

"But what caused the first one?" I asked him as I reluctantly let him help me stand.

He shook his head. "The cause is unknown, but I am sure we will soon find the-" His eyes fell on Herbert and widened. The man's mouth twisted in anger before he threw my hand down and turned to the horsemen. He pointed at her prone body. "Arrest that fiend! This is no doubt her doing!"

I jumped in front of his finger and held up my hands. "Wait a sec! She didn't do anything!"

Renner grasped my shoulders and looked into my eyes. "My Lady, you are new to the city and do not know of its darker places. This fiend-" he nodded at Herbert, "-inhabits one of those darker places."

"But she helped me," I persisted.

Kinos stood. "Lord Renner, I believe there must be some mistake."

Renner looked past me at Kinos and frowned. "There is no mistake. That is Herbert as I live and breathe, and she must be arrested. We will take her ourselves to the prison and you may continue with your work here." Kinos frowned, but bowed his head.

"But she's not the problem!" I insisted as Renner pulled me toward the horses. I yanked myself free from his grasp and stepped back. "The problem is some red-clawed dragon dragged Tillit away and she tried to-" Renner wrapped his hand around my arm.

"A what?" he questioned me.

I leaned away from him and frowned. "A dragon guy kidnapped-"

"We must return to the castle immediately," he insisted.

Renner dragged me over to the horses and placed me in the strong grasp of one of the horsemen. He pushed me onto the saddle of one of the empty steeds while Darda was settled into another. She grabbed her reins and looked forlornly at me as I scowled at Renner.

"If I have any power in this place than you'll leave her alone," I warned him.

He smiled and bowed his head. "I will speak with you when we meet again. Guards, return her to the castle."

One of the horsemen grabbed my reins and turned the horse in the direction of the castle. We galloped away from the devastation, but I caught one last glimpse of the scene over my shoulder. Renner and Kinos stood over Herbert's unconscious form.

I didn't like the pleased look on Renner's face.

CHAPTER 13

My only consolation was the damage to the city was relegated to its most eastern portion. Many of the citizens hurried to the eastern portion with tools and fulcrum supplies to free trapped people and repair the damage. I leaned in the direction they went, but a jarring by my horse brought me back to path.

We soon reached the ship and I was surprised to see Magnus among the men on deck. He bowed his head to me as we walked aboard before he resumed his duties and cast us from the dock. My entourage flanked me on all sides like a tortoise formation that brushed against me every time the ship rocked. Darda stood on the outside of the horsemen with her lips pursed together, and her eyes occasionally flickered to me.

We arrived at the far shore where the entire guard staff waited for us. The long dock was lined with the blue-and-green clad tall dragon-men. Many of them had lengthened hands that ended in sharp dragon talons. I was marched into the castle and up the winding stairs to my chambers with the horsemen in front and behind me. The door was shut behind us and they spread throughout the room. Darda and I were left in the middle of the room.

I turned to her. "I want to know what's going on."

"I am sure you will be allowed an inspection of the damage-" I shook my head.

"Not the mess, but what caused it. Why was Magnus and Kinos so interested in that red dragon guy? And why did Renner give Herbert that ugly look?"

"Herbert is a well-known criminal, My Lady, and Lord Renner has long been eager to capture her," she explained to me as she led us over to the bed. She gestured to the smooth covers. "But would you like to rest?"

I crossed my arms over my chest and planted my feet firmly on the floor. "What about the red dragon? It had the same red scales like the ones that attacked the Portal. Are they connected?"

Darda took a seat on the edge of the bed and pursed her lips. "Undoubtedly."

I arched an eyebrow. "Why undoubtedly?"

She gave a great sigh. "As you have rightly surmised, the red dragons are the Bestia Draconis who sought to destroy the Portal."

I took a seat beside her and looked into her tense face. "Why? Doesn't it help them?"

She shook her head. "No. Their lord and his entire family were destroyed fifty years ago and they were banished from the Continent."

I furrowed my brow. "Fifty years ago? You mean when Xander's mom was killed?"

Darda nodded. "Yes. It was in fact her death that began the Dragon Wars." She closed her eyes and shuddered. "It was a terrible time. The clan of the red dragons swept across the land and burned much of the hinterlands in all the other five realms. It was only through the union wrought by Xander that they were pushed back and eternally banished."

"So that's why Tillit said he wasn't supposed to be down there?" I guessed.

She nodded. "Yes, Mi-My Lady."

I grasped her hands and looked her in the eyes. "Don't go reverting back on me that quick. I'd rather have a friend than a nursemaid."

A ghost of a smile slipped onto her lips as she studied my face. "You are so much like My Lord's mother. She, too, said the same thing to me."

"And I hope you listened to her like you're going to listen to me," I insisted.

She chuckled. "Yes, Miriam."

"And I hope you're going to tell me why a red dragon who's not supposed to be here *is* here," I added.

Darda's face fell and she shook her head. "That I cannot say because I do not know. I am sure Lord Renner-"

She spoke of the devil, and the devil came. The door opened and in stepped my would-be guardian. He shut the door behind him and glanced at the horsemen stationed around the room. They bowed their heads and left the room.

Renner slunk over to us and clasped his hands together. "I hope My Lady is much improved."

I glared at him. "I wasn't that bad in the first place."

He bowed his head. "Perhaps that is true, My Lady, but we could not take any risk."

"Because of the red dragon?" I guessed.

Renner raised his head and showed off his pursed lips. "Beg your pardon, My Lady?"

I waved my hand in the direction of the city. "That Beast Draco or whatever it is. He's why you couldn't take any risk, right?"

"I am sorry you were troubled by the Bestia Draconis, My Lady," he commented as his eyes flickered to Darda. "Perhaps it is best My Lady was allowed to rest and not bothered with these affairs of state."

I leaned to the side and blocked his line of sight to Darda. "If I'm going to be a part of this state than I'm going to need to know what threatens it, and that red dragon definitely looked threatening."

"You needn't worry, My Lady. I am sure he will be found and imprisoned soon," he assured me.

"And Herbert? What about her?" I questioned him.

His smile slipped from his lips. "Your concern for all your subjects is admirable, My Lady, but you needn't worry about the worst of the criminals."

I narrowed my eyes. "Where is she?"

"She is in our custody and is currently recuperating from her injuries," he told me. Renner looked past me at Darda. "Can I trust you to remain with Our Lady while she herself recuperates?"

"I swear My Lady's form will not leave this bed," Darda promised him.

He smiled and bowed his head. "Excellent. Then I will return to the city and look over the damage."

"Isn't that one of my duties?" I piped up.

Renner stepped backward away from the bed and shook his head. "My Lady has been through much, and rest would be more appropriate. Perhaps later, under heavy guard, you will be taken on a tour through the repaired areas."

I tried to stand, but Darda held my shoulders and pressed me down to the bed. I glared at her. "I'd rather go right now. I still have to find Tillit."

She looked me in the eyes and a hint of a smile curled the ends of her lips upward. "My Lady should remain here and rest."

I frowned and looked past her at the movement of Renner closer to the door. He opened the portal and paused in the doorway with the handle in his grasp. "As a precaution, Darda, I will have the horsemen remain in the hallway."

Darda turned to him and frowned. "That is not necessary, Lord Renner."

He chuckled. "But I think it is, Darda. Our Lady could not have escaped from the castle without assistance, and I believe they will act as an efficient deterrent against such foolishness. If you will excuse me there is much work to be done."

The door shut with a clack behind him. I leapt to my feet with my quivering hands balled into fists at my sides. "That asshole's trying to take over the city from me!"

Darda stood and grasped my shoulders before she pressed a finger to her lips. "Lower your voice, Miriam"

"But-" She cupped her palm over my mouth and glanced over her shoulder at the door.

"The guards will become suspicious if you suddenly grow quiet," she told me.

I tore off her hand and glared at her. "What do I care-" She turned back to me and firmly grasped my shoulders.

Her eyes looked deeply into mine. "If you care anything for Tillit you must be quiet," she whispered to me.

I furrowed my brow, but lowered my voice. "Why?"

Darda grabbed my hand and pulled me toward the right-hand wall. "There will be time for questions later, Miriam. For now we must hurry you along to him."

I stumbled after her as we stopped in front of the stone wall. "Hurry along to who?"

Darda released me and pressed her palms against one particular stone. A secret door slid open and revealed a dark, cobweb-filled passage that followed a staircase into a dark abyss. A few forlorn mice scurried away at their revealing, but otherwise the passage was as quiet as a tomb.

I looked to Darda and pointed at the passage. "Does Renner know about this?"

Her eyes twinkled with mischief as she shook her head. "He does not. My Lady-Lady Cate, that is-discovered the passage many years before I became acquainted with her and passed her knowledge on to me."

"So where does this lead? Out of the castle?" I guessed.

"No."

I frowned. "So where does it lead?"

"To the answers you seek, if you are worthy."

I blinked at her. "Come again."

Darda opened her mouth, but a noise from the hall made us both freeze. She half-turned away from me to face the door and lowered her voice to a mere whisper. "You must hurry. Follow the path as far as you must and he will find you."

"Who will-"

"There's no time." She gave me a gentle push into the landing of the passage before the steps.

I caught the wall and stopped before the first step. It was a dark one. "I hope you know what you're talking about. . ." I whispered. My tiny voice echoed down the dark tunnel.

I turned when Darda grasped my hand. She met my eyes and smiled. "There is something I wish to ask you before you leave."

I arched an eyebrow. "What?"

She looked down at her aged hand that held onto mine. "As a girl I was very fond of the nickelodeons. You must promise me you will return and tell me about the movies I have missed."

I returned her smile with one of my own and nodded. "I promise."

Darda let my hand dropped and stepped backward into the room. She pressed on the stone and the door slowly shut.

Darkness closed in on me. Completely, utter darkness. My eyes widened and I lunged for the shrinking escape. "Wait! I need a light!"

She nodded at my pocket. "The stone will-" My hands slapped against the stone as the door shut.

I was alone, and in a very dark place.

CHAPTER 14

I looked over the wall for some sign of light. Nothing broke through the perfect-fitting door. I pounded on the stones, but my only reward was sore fists.

I turned around and leaned my back against the wall. My mind went over Darda's last, interrupted sentence. She'd nodded at the pocket hidden inside the flimsy dress.

That's when it hit me. I dug into my pocket and pulled out the soul stone given to me by the elf king. The stone gave off a soft greenish glow that illuminated the tiny space. I stepped forward and found the stairs. They looked even less inviting in the darkness, but I had a feeling Darda wasn't going to open that door, so I forded on ahead.

The stairs wound down enough floors to reach the courtyard plus one. At the basement level the stairs stopped and a passage begun. By this time I was dizzy from so many corners. I barely knew my left from my right, much less which direction the passage now led me. Part of me hoped it was the lake where I could hitch a ride from Magnus. Another part told me Renner know doubt had guards everywhere long the dock. My last part reminded me I was hungry.

Wherever I traveled, it felt like forever. My footsteps clacked against the lonely cobblestones as my small light lit up the gray stone walls. They reminded me of the hidden passages beneath the city.

"I wonder if Tillit knows about this. . ." I murmured. My heart sank as I thought about my enterprising friend. "I wonder where he is. . ."

I froze. A light had appeared ahead of me like someone had turned on a light switch. The white beam traveled down the passage and stopped just short of where I stood. It flickered like candlelight and beckoned me to come. I didn't need a second invitation.

I raced down the passage and saw the light came from an open doorway. That must have been why it appeared so suddenly. I burst through the doorway and onto a balcony. A long drop in front of me made me put on the brakes, but I still slammed into the black metal railing. I grabbed the top and stared down into another world.

Beneath me were a dozen circular balconies like the one on which I found myself. Every floor was covered in bookcases, and their shelves were packed with books. I tilted my head back and saw the same view, and above the final floor was a glass dome through which shone natural sunlight. It was that light that had brought me to this strange place.

The balcony I found myself on had a walkway that extended to a circular platform in the center of the floor. In the middle, placed high on a pedestal, was a giant globe of a world. The blue and green paints of water and earth shone beneath the direct light from above.

I kept my hold on the railing and followed it onto the walkway and to the center platform. A tap on the floor told me the platform was steady, so I took a deep breath and let go of the railing.

I turned in a circle and swept my eyes over the massive library. There must have been hundreds of shelves with thousands of books. The countless, colorful spines shone in the brilliant light that pierced the glass dome. An aroma of old pages filled my nostrils. Clouds drifted over the sky and caused the sun to flicker like dancing pixies over the books.

"It is rather peaceful, is it not?"

My heart skipped a beat before I spun around. There, standing three feet shy of me and blocking the catwalk, was a small, hunched man. He appeared to be fifty and wore a heavy pair of spectacles on his thin nose. His hands were clasped behind his back and opened his flowing gray robe to reveal a simple tunic underneath. A smile danced across his lips as he shuffled over to stand beside me before the globe.

"I apologize if I startled you. I receive visitors so rarely that I sometimes forget my manners," he told me.

I took a step back. "Who are you?"

He set his palm against the globe and stared at me out of the corner of his eyes. "Who am I? You do not ask where you are?"

I frowned. "Aren't we in the castle at Alexandria?"

The man tilted his head back and nodded at the glass dome. "Do you believe that is the skies of Alexandria?"

I followed his gaze and pursed my lips. "Well, if we're not there then where are we?"

LABYRINTH OF THE DRAGON

I stepped back as he slipped around the globe past me and walked a quarter the way around the globe before he stopped before a large land mass. "This place is where one needs to be when a worthy one asks a worthy question."

I raised an eyebrow. "Come again?"

The man smiled. "You are at the library of Mallus. I am its librarian, and my name is Crates."

I blinked at him. "Like the box?"

Crates bowed his head. "Precisely." He straightened and cleared his throat. "But where are my manners? If you are here than surely you have a very important question to ask me?"

I furrowed my brow and stared hard at the base of the globe. "I do?"

"Did you not ask yourself a question before you noticed the light from the doorway?" he wondered.

My eyes widened and I snapped my fingers. "I did! I was wondering where Tillit was!"

Crates chuckled and slowly spun the globe. "You ask a very simple question. Is he very important to you? A friend, perhaps? Or a lover?"

I cringed. "Definitely friend, but I owe him one. He saved my life."

His smile softened as he studied me. "Then we will have to find this precious friend of yours."

The old man stopped his spinning of the globe and pressed his palm against the large land mass. The mass burst upward into the air above the globe like a clear hologram. My eyes widened as I recognized the High Castle and the woods of Viridi Silva. A tiny trail of blue light led from the castle through the woods to the city of Alexandria.

I pointed at the line and looked to the old man. "How do you know I went that way?"

"There is very little information not found in Mallus," he told me. His hand hovered over the globe and twitched his fingers. The holographic map zoomed in to Alexandria and Beriadan Lake. The picture was so clear I could see the sparkle of the skies in the smooth surface of the waters. "It appears your friend is somewhere below the lake."

"How do you know that? How do you know anything?" I persisted.

He dropped his hand to his side. The image over the glow disappeared. Crates turned and studied me with a mischievous smile. "This library is rather unusual. You see, it is of the world, and yet has no place within the world."

I blinked at him. "Come again?"

He raised his eyes to the bright ceiling. "To be concise, the library floats through time and space without anchor, but not without purpose." He returned his gaze to me and smiled. "It comes to the call of any who needs it vast collection of books, and my knowledge."

"So it kind of floats everywhere?" I guessed.

He bowed his head. "In a way, yes."

"And knows everything?"

"Nearly so."

"So could it tell me why I've got fae powers?" I wondered.

He chuckled. "There are some things in this world best learned not through a book, but through life. Otherwise, life would be very dull." He tilted his head to one side as though listening to a sound I couldn't hear. His eyebrows crashed down and his lips pursed together. "While I would very much like to continue this conversation, it appears the friend you seek is in grave danger. He needs your help most urgently, or he will die."

My heart skipped a beat. "Tillit?"

He righted his head and nodded. "Yes. His captors mean to kill him."

My eyes widened. "But how do I save him? I don't know where he is!"

He slipped beside me to set his hand on the small of my back and studied my face. "I will take you very close to him, but are you sure you wish to attempt a rescue? His captors are very powerful, and behind them lies a great shadow."

"I've got to try," I insisted.

He smiled. "An excellent answer. Come."

Crates led me across the catwalk and over to the door through which I'd entered. It was shut now. He grasped the knob and pushed me toward the entrance.

His eyes met mine. "Fare you well, Neito Vedesta, and may your line run long."

I pointed at the door. "That's the door I came in. How's that going to get me to Tillit?"

"Like this."

Crates opened the door and shoved me through the doorway. I stumbled not into the dark world of the passage, but into the bright blue world of the secret tunnels beneath the lake and city. My shoulder hit one of the blue walls and I spun around to face the door.

It was gone. There was only a narrow hallway of blue stone that disappeared around a bend.

"You're very troublesome."

That voice. That was the red-handed dragon speaking. I spun around and looked in the opposite direction.

"I try to make things interesting for my murderers."

Tillit!

CHAPTER 15

I stuck to one side of the passage and crept forward. The voices came from a bend in the tunnel. I peeked around the turn and saw it led into a small, round chamber. The backs of the sus and their dragon leader were turned to me. In front of them and seated on the ground was Tillit. He sported a black eye and scuffs on his cheeks. His arms and legs were tied behind him with thick rope.

The clothes of the entire company were disheveled and a thin layer of dust that powdered their clothes with a brown tinge of color.

Tillit smiled up at the dragon leader. One of his lips was cracked and bleeding. "You should treat your swine some manners. I think I blacked out back there."

The dragon returned his smile with a grin of his own. "I'm afraid that was the point. You know these tunnels very well, but not even you are familiar with this part. We didn't want to change that."

I looked around my feet for something to throw at the crowd. Maybe I could return the favor for Tillit.

A pair of strong arms grabbed mine and yanked them behind me. I yelped and thrashed in their clutches, but they wrapped a rough rope around my wrists and pushed me forward. I stumbled into the chamber. The group spun around. The color drained from Tillit's face when he saw me.

"I got that extra rope you wanted, Boss, but I had to use it," my captor informed his leader.

The dragon studied me and a crooked, lecherous smile slipped onto his lips. "That's quite all right." He stepped up to me and clasped my chin between his hands to force me to look into his face. "You've caught a nice fish in these watery tunnels."

I wrenched my chin from his grip and glared at him. "What the hell are you doing down here? Don't you know these tunnels are off-limits to visitors?"

He chuckled. "The tunnels handle themselves well enough with all these twists and turns." He stepped closer to me so our chests nearly bumped into one another. His red-colored eyes looked down and studied my face. "But I wonder how a pretty little thing like you got down here. Were you perhaps following someone?"

I looked away and shrugged. "I was just walking around when I heard voices. That's it. So are you going to let me go or not?"

He half-turned and looked to Tillit. "You don't look so well, Tillit. Do you know this girl?"

Tillit scoffed. "Never seen her before in my life."

The dragon's eyes flickered to me. "That's a pity."

LABYRINTH OF THE DRAGON

He looked past me at the sus who captured me and nodded. The sus wrapped one pudgy arm around my upper chest and pulled my back against the front of his dusty shirt. He drew out a long knife and pressed the blade against my throat.

"Wait!" Tillit shouted.

The dragon looked back to him. "I knew you were soft on children, but soft on strange women?"

"She's my assistant, but she doesn't know what's going on, so just let her go," he insisted.

The leader of the gang laughed as the knife was removed from my throat. "Sentimental people really are fools. She knows how to get here, thus she knows how to get out." He turned to us and jerked his head toward Tillit. "Put her beside her boss."

The sus shoved me forward. I stumbled and fell onto my knees beside Tillit. His eyes flickered to me. "You shouldn't have come," he whispered.

"You're telling me. . ." I mumbled as my legs were bound.

I heard a scuff and looked over my shoulder. Several of the sus were leaving the chamber. Only the dragon and one other sus remained.

"You're just going to leave us here to die?" I questioned him.

The dragon knelt in front of me and his cruel smile widened. "Take heart, little assistant. We won't submit such a beautiful creature to such a terrible death." He nodded at the blue walls. "These walls have a unique feature. They are as strong as the toughest sword in keeping back water." His last man stepped up to a wall and produced a chisel and hammer from his coat. He placed the chisel against the wall and knocked the head of the hammer against the flat top. Hairline cracks spread from the point of impact and several feet across the wall. "Unfortunately, against the tools of civilization they are as weak as glass."

"Then you've got a lot of faith in thinking that sword is real," Tillit wondered.

The man stood and stared down at us. "Let's just say I have it on good authority that the legends are more than just legends. You could have made it easier for us, and yourself, of course, by helping us, but I think we'll manage without your knowledge." An audible cracking noise came from the wall at which the henchman chinked The red dragon stepped back and bowed to us. "But if you will excuse us, we have a flood to escape. I hope you know how to swim."

His piggish cohorts laughed as they left the chamber. I heard more chinking from the chisel followed by the unmistakable sound of a cave-in. Then all was quiet.

"The fools are smarter than I thought blocking the tunnel. . ." Tillit muttered.

I whipped my head to Tillit who was squirming. "I hope you have a plan to get us out of here."

He furrowed his brow as he twisted his bound arms. "My plan is to get my hands loose and get us untied."

"And how's that going?"

"Not too great."

Another cracking noise warned us of impending doom. My pulse quickened as I returned my sights to the damaged wall. A little bit of water leaked through the cracks. "You might want to work faster."

"I don't have dragon strength, and sus make the best knots," he told me.

LABYRINTH OF THE DRAGON

I swept my eyes over the chamber. There wasn't a single sharp stone to be had other than the shattered pieces of wall. "What I wouldn't do for a good knife right now, or even a hammer."

Tillit paused and his eyes widened. He looked to me and jerked his head at the mound of shattered blue stone. "Can you grab one of those pieces with your teeth?"

I blinked at him, but nodded. "Yeah, but-"

"There's no time. Grab it and knock the piece against the wall." He resumed his struggles with his ropes. "I'll try to get myself free."

I rolled over to the pile of rock. The blue stones sat in a nice puddle, and it was like bobbing for apples trying to get one between my teeth. The water over my head became a steady stream. By the time I clamped my teeth on a large stone and sat up I was soaked.

"Tho Ah puth this againth the vall?" I asked Tillit.

He nodded. "Yes. Tap against it as loud as you can. With any luck he'll hear you."

I blinked at him. "Who will hear me?"

He glared at me. "Tap before that wall collapses!"

I tapped the longest end of the stone against the wall. Flakes fell away from both wall and stone as more water poured into the chamber. The floor filled with the cold liquid and reached up over our ankles.

"Damn it!" Tillit cursed. "The water's on the rope!"

I shifted the rock in my mouth. The water made the stone slippery and it fell with a 'plop' into the pool below me. "Whatever this is supposed to do it isn't working!"

"Then use your head!" he insisted.

"What the hell am I doing this for?" I snapped.

Tillit nodded at the dark water beyond the blue transparent stone. "Beriadan is in that lake somewhere, and if you're really a mare fae he's bound to come rescue-" Part of the wall above me gave way.

A torrential waterfall crashed into the chamber. Within ten seconds there was a foot of water around us, and more was coming in at a faster rate.

"Lean against the wall and try to stand!" Tillit ordered me.

I leaned against the wall, but another crack broke open beside me. The new waterfall slammed into me and sent me head-first into the rising water. I twisted and turned, and saw Tillit's shadowy, warped figure against the wall.

"Miriam!" came his voice through the water.

I tried to swing my legs beneath me, but the swirling current pushed me around the floor of the chamber. My shoulder slammed into the exterior wall. The knock forced the air from my lungs. Little bubbles of breath floated out of me and were caught in the rough current and swept out through a hole. My vision grew blurry as the air in my lungs depleted.

Please not this way. I don't want to die like this. Not without seeing Xander one last time.

The remainder of the wall collapsed beneath the onslaught of water eager to spill into the chamber. Tillit was forced under water, and I watched him writhe as he fought against our fate.

A bright color caught my dimming attention. It was blue, but not like the walls. This blue contained its own light, and that light grew brighter as it approached me. It was a band of blue light like I'd seen in the Potami River, but the stream was much longer and thicker. The light was so bright I could barely look at it.

The band slipped around Tillit and me and engulfed us in a soft warmth. A pocket of air wrapped around my head. I gasped and coughed out the water that had nearly filled my lungs to the brim. The band pulled us out of the drowned chamber and into the darkness of the lake. Rather than rising, we were pulled downward into the depths of the deep, dark water.

CHAPTER 16

Tillit floated close to me. His face sported a wide grin as he nodded at the opposite end of the band. I followed his nod and glimpsed a shadowy, transparent form at the other end of the light. It was that of a tall man clad in a cloak the color of the darkness around us. A hood covered his head, but a long black beard of moss and wavy hair trailed behind him. The lower half of his body disappeared into the band that held onto us. He faced away from us as he pulled us down into the unfathomable depths of the lake.

We reached the bottom of the lake and floated across the bed. The band of light illuminated about twenty feet all around us and allowed us to see a mingled world of nature and civilization. Long strips of seaweed waved at us, and at their bases were the wrecks of hundreds of ships. The cargo of those ships was endless. Ancient statutes stared into the darkness ahead of them, countless pieces of jars were strewn about, and here and there was a large crate pushed overboard for some flaw or to escape inspection.

We crested the lake floor and found ourselves looking down into a large, jagged hole. The roughly circular area was a hundred feet below the rest of the floor. The tall walls of the hole cast their dark shadows over a large galleon that sat in the center of the area. The tall, unbroken masts rose up like the spires of the city.

We slipped through a gaping hole in the side and into the cargo hold. Broken crates and barrels still sat where the crew had set them. A group of chests sat against the back wall. Their precious load of gold coins, gems, and precious stones was spilled onto the planks and dazzled in the light of the blue band.

Seated in the center of the fortune was a tall throne of gold. An arch of diamonds decorated the tall back, and the end of the arms was covered in silver plating. Our spectral-like guide turned and seated himself on the throne. He drew back his hood and revealed himself to be a pale man of about forty-five. His hands grasped the arms and his form became less transparent. Tillit and I floated to within five feet of him so he could study us with his bright blue eyes.

When he spoke his voice was as deep as the call of the waves in a storm, but had the gentle touch of the lapping waters against the shore. "It is many ages since I met one with whom I could claim kinship. Who is your parent, little niece?"

I swallowed the lump in my throat and shook my head. "I-I don't know."

A soft smile slipped onto his lips. "You needn't fear me, young one. I mean you no harm, but merely wish to know another of the Mare Fae."

Tillit raised his hand. "Not to interrupt this heartfelt family get-together, but we need to get to the surface as soon as possible or you'll be receiving a lot of visitors."

The fae arched an eyebrow. "How so?"

Tillit pointed a finger at the darkness above us. "That wall that broke on us is just the start of everyone's problems. Those guys aren't going to stop until they've got that sword."

Beriadan frowned and rose to his feet. "Of what sword do you speak?"

The sus grinned. "You know the one I'm meaning. You helped make it."

Beriadan tilted his head back and looked up at the ceiling of the hold. "I understand."

"I don't," I spoke up. I looked from the water god to the two-footed hog. "What are you two talking about? What sword?"

"That's the sword old Darda told you about earlier, the one your husband's ancestor hid away," Tillit told me. He jerked his head in the direction of the surface. "Those guys who tried to make us into fishes are after it, and they're not afraid to bust the whole tunnel system wide open to get at it."

"Have they discovered its resting spot?" Beriadan asked him.

Tillit nodded. "I think so, at least they're pretty sure it it. That's why we've got to get up there right now, or not even your crest is going to be able to save a house."

Beriadan arched an eyebrow. "They are the source of the earthquake that shook my city?"

LABYRINTH OF THE DRAGON

"Yep, and there's going to be a lot more of those if we don't get up there," Tillit warned him.

"Then I will send you there at once."

Beriadan raised one of his hands so his palm faced us. A rush of water flew from his palm and swept past Tillit and me. The water arced upward and opened the hatch above our heads. The blue light around us shaped itself into two bubbles, one for each of us, and we floated toward the opening.

I pressed my palms against the front of my bubble and looked down at Beriadan. "Wait a sec!" Our bubbles jerked to a stop and he met my gaze. "Can you tell me anything about myself? Like how I'm a fae?"

He floated up to me and pressed his hands against the bubble opposite where mine lay. A soft glow emanated from both our palms and I felt a warmth slip into me like when that phantom version of me had slipped into me after I saved the forest prince, Durion.

Beriadan leaned toward me and lowered his voice to a whisper I barely heard. "If you wish to know yourself, seek out Valtameri. He will know your lineage."

I blinked at him. "Seek out-" Beriadan floated away and the light died between us.

A soft smile graced his lips as he studied me. "Keep yourself safe, little one. So few of us remain."

I banged on the wall of my bubble. "Hey! Wait a-ah!" Our bubbles shot upward through the hatch and out into the open lake water.

The force of the blast was enough to knock me off my feet. I fell flat on my butt onto the bottom of the bubble and clung to the wet floor.

"Don't hold on to the bubble too tight!" Tillit warned me.

I whipped my head to him. "Why?"

He nodded at the fast-approaching light that marked the surface. Everything sped by us at near light-speed. "Because the magic of a mare fae is limited to the water. Once we break through the surface they're going to disappear."

My eyes widened. "And then what?"

"Then we swim."

"But I can't swim!"

"Then now would be an excellent time to learn."

We shot out of the water and high into the air in an arc. The bubbles around us popped and we flailed our arms as though we could fly. The dark blue water below us changed to the wooden planks of a familiar ship. We dropped from the sky and landed with a hard thump onto the deck.

Tillit sat up and winced as his back cracked. "Beriadan has excellent aim, but I wish the landing would have been gentler."

A pair of feet walked up to me. I looked up into the curious face of Magnus. Behind him stood Kinos with his hawk on his shoulder.

"By the gods, but where did you come from?" Magnus asked us.

I sat up and rubbed my bruised arms. "Would you believe in the company of a lake god?"

He nodded. "Aye, Ah would, but how did you come to be down there?"

"And where have you been for this long day?" Kinos spoke up.

I blinked at him. "What day?"

LABYRINTH OF THE DRAGON

"Lord Renner informed us of your disappearance from the castle a day ago. He imprisoned Darda for her assisting in your escape and called a search for you. Nothing was found these last twenty-four hours," he explained.

I stood on my shaky legs and clutched my head. "I don't know. I got into this weird library, and then the old man shoved me through a door into a tunnel beneath the city where I found Tillit, then we were almost drowned by a bunch of sus and that red dragon but Beriadan saved us, and now we're here."

"And regretfully, we're going to need to talk to Renner," Tillit spoke up as he joined our little circle. He looked from Magnus to Kinos. "That damn red dragon is out to get Bucephalus."

The men started back. "*The* Bucephalus?" Kinos asked him.

Tillit glared at him. "Do you think I'm making this up to amuse myself?"

I stepped into the fray and held up my hands. "Wait a minute. So what if this dragon guy gets a hold of this busuffering-thing?"

"The legends that surround Bucephalus say it was an indestructible sword that could cut through anything," Kinos told me.

Magnus nodded. "Aye, 'twould be trouble in the hands of the likes of that fellow."

I let my arms drop to my sides and my face fell. "So it'd be like giving a grenade to a psychopath?"

Kinos shook his head. "I know not what a 'grenade' is, but we cannot let such a weapon be used by any of the Bestia."

Magnus nodded and looked up at the helmsman. "Set course for the-" A low, deep rumble interrupted his order.

CHAPTER 17

The trees in the near city rattled their branches together and the ground shook. A great cry of fear arose from the streets and buildings. The containers at the port danced atop one another. Men grabbed onto the posts to keep from falling into the lake.

Small waves rose up from the once-placid lake water and rocked the boat until I felt like a rubber ducky in a hurricane. The waves grew larger as the rumbling grew louder. I tripped and would have fallen if Kinos hadn't caught me.

He looked to Magnus. "To the castle, captain!"

"There's no time for that!" Tillit yelled as he stumbled against the railing. He pointed at the shrine fifty yards off from the port side. "Get us to the island!"

Magnus limped up the stairs to the wheel and shoved the helmsman from his post. He turned the wheel a sharp left and looked down at the crew, Nimeni among them. "Open the blasted sails!"

The men scrambled for the ropes and climbed the rigging to the sails. The white canvas opened all at once and we put on a burst of speed toward the island.

"By the gods, what was that?" Kinos wondered as he released me and hurried to the railing.

Tillit already leaned over the railing and looked behind us. I hurried to their side and followed their gaze. Behind us was a large, permanent wave. The three-foot tall wall of water pushed against the rear of our ship and shoved us forward. A soft blue light illuminated the center of the wave.

Tillit laughed and slapped the top of the railing. "Now that's a god I can get behind!"

"Or in front of," I quipped.

We covered the short distance in even shorter time. The pushy wave beached the small ship several yards onto the sand and the plank was lowered. Tillit hurried down the wood, and behind him came Kinos and myself. The tremors were less severe, but continued with a horrible consistency.

Magnus limped down the stairs and looked to Nimeni. "Ah can't keep the pace, so you go along and help 'em!"

Nimeni nodded and rushed after us as we sprinted toward the temple. Kumartua the half-fae stepped out of the shrine and, upon seeing our group, slammed the door shut behind him. He just finished locking the handles with a heavy chain and bolt when we arrived.

"Open the door!" Tillit ordered him.

Kumartua turned around and glared at him as he tucked the key into his vest. "You have no right to order me about.

LABYRINTH OF THE DRAGON

As keeper of the shrine I have full discretion to shut the shrine whenever I deem it necessary."

Nimeni strode through our group and Kumartua scuttled out of his way. The pale man grabbed the chain, and the hunchback sneered at him. "You fool. That chain was forged from the hardest metal. No one can-" Nimeni pulled the chain in opposite directions. Two of the links snapped, and the chain fell broken to the ground. Kumartua stared with wide eyes at his fallen deterrent. "B-but-"

"We don't have time for your jabbering," Tillit commented as he shoved Kumartua out of the way.

He flung the doors open and guided us over to the statue. A quick tap of the hand and the secret entrance opened.

"By all the gods. . ." Kinos murmured.

"No, just one, now quickly," Tillit replied as he rushed down the steps.

Tillit led us into the bright blue tunnels of the ancient dragons and enterprising sus. We swept through the catacomb chamber and into the never-ending labyrinth. Tillit made countless turns left and right as we sped our way through the blue-lit passages.

"Are you sure you know the way?" Kinos spoke up.

A huge explosion echoed down the tunnel and was soon followed by another violent earthquake. We hit the walls as the blue stone walls cracked and bits fell from the ceiling. The shaking stopped, but we all knew that wouldn't last long.

Tillit looked up at the ceiling and pursed his lips. "I'm betting my life on it."

We resumed our run through the maze of tunnels. The walls slowly changed from the blue color to the hard gray.

The passages grew so narrow the broader-shouldered men had to turn at an angle, slowing down our progress. Hope was renewed when I noticed footprints in the dust of the little-used passage.

We reached a sharp bend on the passage when Tillit came to a sudden stop. Kinos knocked into his back and I knocked into Kinos's. Nimeni was the only balanced one of our group not to join the conga line of dumb.

I looked ahead at Tillit. "What's the-" He pressed a finger against his lips before he used the same finger to point at the way ahead of us.

My weak ears heard the faint sound of voices. Tillit hunched close to the ground and slunk forward. We mimicked his walking style and soon came to another sharp bend. Beyond the corner the tunnel opened to a large chamber. It was much like the tomb chamber, but four times as large and only the left half of the area was in the blue stone. The other half was the gray rough stone of the mountains. In the center of the room was an altar that looked like a bird bath. A fish and dragon rose from the center of the bowl and twined around one another.

The sacred place was a mess. Bits of rubble were strewn about the floor. The blue-stone wall was cracked, and the gray rock wall was full of jagged, gaping holes. The culprits stood in the mouth of one of the larger holes and peeked inside. It was the group of sus, and at their head was the red dragon.

He peeked into the wreckage and scowled. "More rock. Where the hell can it be?"

"Maybe it's not real," one of the sus suggested.

LABYRINTH OF THE DRAGON

The dragon looked over his shoulder and sneered at the sus. "Did you forget about the old map the hunchback found? It led us here."

"But maybe it's not here anymore," another sus spoke up.

The dragon snarled and marched over to the altar. He grasped the edges and looked at the entwined figures. "It has to be here. Otherwise this chamber would not have been so well hidden and blocked."

"But we can't do much more blasting, boss," the first sus commented as he pointed at the cracked ceiling. "This place is ready to fall apart."

The dragon spun around and faced them. "We will do as much blasting as must be done! Whatever it takes we will find that sword!"

Tillit stepped into the chamber and cleared his throat. Our foes whipped their heads to him as he made a sweeping bow. "Good evening, gentlemen. It's a pleasure to see you again."

One of the sus pointed a shaking finger at him. "I-it's a ghost!"

"Then catch it and sell it!" the dragon ordered him.

The thought of such a prize swept away all fear from the enterprising sus, and they charged Tillit. Nimeni, Kinos and his hawk flew past me and into the fray. The sus were powerful creatures, but against the trained soldier and the experienced sailor, plus Tillit, they found their match.

While the men proceeded to beat the crap out of each other, I saw movement beyond them. The dragon boy slipped over to a large sack and pulled out a ball. The round object had two compartments, and in each compartment was a liquid, one black and the other brown.

He raised the ball above his head and looked like he meant to throw it to the floor. My tingling survival sense told me that wouldn't have been a good idea, so I rushed through the thicket of the fighting and tackled the dragon. Sort of.

I slammed into his arm and knocked the ball loose. It hit him on the head on its way down and fell harmlessly to the ground. He grabbed the collar of my dress with his now-free hand and lifted me so we were face-to-face. His red eyes burned into mine as his lips curled back to reveal long, sharp dragon teeth. He opened his wide jaws and meant to sink those teeth into my neck.

One of the sus slammed into both of us. The red dragon and his minion tumbled into the far corner of the chamber while I rolled into the base of the altar. Kinos hurried over and knelt in front of me with a worried expression on his face.

"A thousand pardons, My Lady. I meant only to throw him into the man," he explained.

I sat up and rubbed my bruised head, but managed to give him a smile. "That's okay. I think his bite was going to be worse than your aim."

He grinned and helped me to my feet. I looked at our other two companions. Nimeni stood over our unconscious foes who sat on the ground against the blown gray wall. Tillit finished the last of the rope binding, using their own rope that lay near the wall, and stood.

He turned to us and wiped his hands together to clean them of the dust. "Well, that was exciting. Now let's see about that map."

He strode over to the bag at my feet and rummaged through the contents. In a short while he produced a rolled up piece of aged parchment and carefully unrolled it on the floor. It revealed a map of the labyrinth. There was the entrance through the shrine and the long tunnels we followed to get to the chamber in which we found ourselves. The gray wall existed because the chamber lay at along the shore and against the foot of the mountains.

Tillit brushed his hand against over the altar chamber. "There has to be something in here to show us the way."

I looked up and studied the statues. The fish and dragon wound around one another, but I noticed their eyes both faced one direction: the rear wall of the chamber. It was the point where the gray rock met the blue stone. There was a jagged connection from the floor to the ceiling. I walked over to the point and brushed my hand against the blue wall.

I started back when my palm glowed. There was a matching glow from behind the wall. It followed the jagged connection from the floor to a foot above me. My hand and the wall didn't stop glowing.

I looked over my shoulder. "Um, guys? I think I found something."

CHAPTER 18

The men stood and walked over to me. Tillit pressed his hand against the wall and peeked into the crack. A grin spread across his lips. "My dear Miriam, it looks like you've found just what we're looking for. Everyone stand back."

We moved back and Tillit pressed his palm against various spots in the wall. One of them did the trick because the wall swung open in two parts. There, wrapped in a thick mess of rope and standing upright with the point downward, was a large sword. The hilt was made of steel and wrapped with a green leather cloth. The blade itself was white with a bluish tinge that reflected the glow in my hands. The pure sword reflected our awed faces.

I looked from one to the other of my companions. "So how do we get it out?"

LABYRINTH OF THE DRAGON

Tillit stepped forward and tapped on the rope with his finger. A spark of blue light sizzled at the point of contact. He winced and yanked his hand away. "A sword won't cut through it, that's for sure." He turned to me and looked down. A smile slipped onto his lips. "But I think I might know what will."

I followed his gaze to my glowing hands. I stepped back and shook my head. "Oh no, not me."

He stepped aside and nodded. "Yes, you. The sword wants someone

"Can you be sure of that?" Kinos challenged him.

Tillit shrugged. "Nope, but I don't have anything to lose, and a little zap isn't going to hurt her."

Kinos frowned. "I would rather we think of a different-"

"I'll do it." The men turned to me. I shrugged. "Or at least I'll try. It won't hurt much if it fails, right?"

My heart sank a little when they didn't reply, but rather Kinos and Tillit glanced at each other. I steadied myself and walked through them up to the sword. The blue hue on the blade glowed brighter as I raised my hand even with the hilt. I shut my eyes and wrapped my hand around the soft cloth.

No zap. No tingle. Nothing. I creaked open my eyes and looked at the sword. It was still stuck in the rope.

My face fell and I looked to Tillit. "How am I-" I pulled my lazy arm with me and the blade sliced clean through the rope. The loss of stability made me stumble back and the point of the sword clunked onto the ground in front of me.

Everyone, myself included, stared at the sword for a moment with wide eyes. Then Tillit lifted his face and clapped his hands. "Excellent! A wonderful cut!"

I sheepishly grinned and raised the sword a little off the floor. That's all I could do. The thing was as heavy as a rock, and nearly three feet long. The blade reflected the room perfectly, and it also reflected the figure of the red dragon as he crawled toward the dropped ball.

I swung around a half second after my protectors as they, too, noticed our not-so-fallen foe climb to his feet. He snarled at us as he drew back his hand that clutched the grenade-like ball. "No one will have it!" he proclaimed as he lobbed the weapon.

Kinos and Nimeni leapt in front of Tillit and me to block the weapon, but my reach was just a little longer. I grabbed the hilt with both hands and swung the blade upward. The ball started its downward arc when it was sliced neatly in two by the sword. Its liquid splashed across the floor in front of our group, and wherever they combined there was a huge explosion.

The blast knocked us back. I slammed into the far wall and Tillit was beside me. Kinos and Nimeni rolled a little before they caught themselves in a crouched position. A familiar cracking noise above our heads signaled danger. We whipped our heads up and watched a hairline fracture open into a full-fledged problem. The earth shook as bits of the ceiling crashed down on us.

Kinos and Nimeni turned toward the wall and rushed over to me. They both slammed their palms against the wall above my head and covered me with their bodies. I would have been flattered if I hadn't been so scared as the ceiling caved in on us with a great deafening roar. The chamber darkened as a thick layer of dust spread over the blue walls. Far-off, muffled screams came to my ears. Maybe some of them were mine. I couldn't be sure.

LABYRINTH OF THE DRAGON

The earthquake lasted as long as the cave-in, and that felt like forever. Finally the rumbling and roaring stopped. I choked on the thick film of dust that floated over the once-mighty chamber. Two bodies shifted above me. I peeked open my eyes. Kinos and Nimeni shrugged the small rocks off their shoulders and straightened. Kinos's small hawk shook the dust from its wings and glared at everything. Above them was the dim light of the early morning sky.

"What a fanatic!" Tillit grumbled as he emerged from a pile of rubble. He stepped out from his hide-away hole and climbed over the debris to us. "Everything has to be all-or-nothing with them. They even have to make their death a huge ordeal for everyone else."

Kinos looked over his shoulder at where our foe had stood and frowned. "He is not dead."

A large pile of debris burst asunder and a great shadow emerged from the fallen stones. It was the red dragon, but he was no longer in his human form. He stood two stories tall and was covered in scales of such a deep red they were nearly black. Wafts of smoke puffed out from the nostrils of his long snout and his red, slitted eyes glared down at us. He bashed his tail against the wall behind him and shook the ruins of the chamber.

Kinos whipped his head to Nimeni. "Get her out of-" The red dragon roared and charged through the debris toward us. The men and hawk stiffened for combat as our foe leaned down to snap us up in his jaws.

A shadow fell through the open ceiling and landed atop the red dragon. Our foe's face slammed into the rocks and his jaws snapped shut with a hard clack. The shadow lifted its head and let out a roar that shook the walls.

I had seen that green dragon once before, at the Portal that led to my old world. My knight in scaled armor had come to save me.

CHAPTER 19

Xander climbed off our foe and stomped over to us. Nimeni and Kinos parted so my dragon lord could reach me. He leaned his long neck down and bumped his nose against me. I smiled and patted his nose. My other hand held the hilt of the heavy sword that dragged the ground.

Xander's eyes flitted down to the sword. His green eyes widened. I followed his gaze and nodded. "Yep. It's Bucephalus."

Xander turned to Kinos. "It is true, My-" A sharp hiss caught our attention.

The red dragon stood up and snapped his jaws at Xander's hindquarters. Xander swung around and whacked his tail across the red dragon's face. Our foe flew back and toppled into the opposite wall. Xander charged the red dragon and pinned him to the ground with one of his clawed hands. He leaned down and curled his lips back in a snarl.

The red dragon grinned. His deep, growling voice laughed. "You think you're having the sword will make any difference? My lord will make sure it doesn't." He clamped down on something in his mouth.

A small explosion went off that blew apart his head and sent Xander stumbling away. Blood and gore splashed over the chamber walls and floors. We were not spared. A nice glob smacked onto my chest and slid down my front before it dropped to the ground at my feet.

The headless dragon body fell limp over the debris and lay still. I wish I could have said the same thing about my heart.

Xander stood and glared at his suicidal foe before he turned to us. "Are you all well?"

We nodded. I winced as I looked over the blood-red walls of the formerly majestic altar chamber. "This is going to take a lot of soap water."

Xander partially climbed out of the hole, but hung his tail over the edge into the chamber. His scaly rear wrapped itself around me and pulled me out of the subterranean world and into the light of the rising sun. I blinked against the soft glow as people emerged from the local buildings and streets. That's when I realized the hole stood in the square in front of the Sus Tavi.

Xander pulled Tillit out, and the sus walked up to the front door. He put his hands on his hips and grinned up at the sign. "I always knew this was a sacred place."

The last of us was pulled out and Xander reverted back to his human form. I was surprised to see his body was covered by a thin bit of cloth. He walked over to me and held out his hands. "May I?"

I blinked at him before I realized he wanted the sword. "O-oh! Right! Sure, it's yours, after all." I handed the sword to him. He took it in one hand and sliced the air, creating a faint whistling noise. "Magnificent. . ." he murmured.

I pointed at him. "And doesn't explain how you're here. Aren't you supposed to be somewhere south?"

He lowered the sword and nodded. "Yes, but I received the message from Kinos's eagle a half day ago and flew here as fast as I could manage."

I turned to Kinos. "You have an eagle?"

He pursed his lips and nodded. "Yes, but that was very reckless of you, My Lord," he commented as he walked up to us. His eyes studied Xander's body. Even I noticed his tense, sweat covered muscles. "I never intended for you to return through the air. The strain might have been too much for you."

Xander looked to me. "To fail to reach here would have been a far greater pain." He winced and clutched his chest as his legs wobbled beneath him.

"Xander!" I yelled as I caught him under one arm.

He gave me a shaky smile. "My apologies. The strain of the transformation was more than I anticipated."

Kinos slipped beneath Xander's other arm and bore the full brunt of the heavy burden. "We should get you to the castle, My Lord."

A thundering of hooves signaled just such a help. A group of familiar riders stampeded down the main street and up to us. My face fell when I recognized Renner at the head. He leapt off his horse and threw the reins to another rider before he hurried to Xander.

Renner knelt down and bowed his head. "My Lord! You have returned at our hour of need!"

Xander gently removed himself from Kinos's hold, and stood straight and tall. He swept a hand over our small group. "On the contrary, I have come only to congratulate the true heroes of the city."

Renner raised his head and his eyes fell on me. "My Lady! You have been found! But where have you been?"

I crossed my arms and glared at him. "In a safe place, and now that I'm found you can let Darda out of the dungeon now."

Xander frowned and looked to Renner. "What is the meaning of this?"

Renner groveled before our lord. "My Lady went missing, and the old retainer refused to tell us where she had gone, so I-" Xander raised his hand.

"I do not fully understand the situation, but whatever intentions Darda had for hiding my lady they could not have been for ill. She is to be released at once."

Renner smiled and nodded. "Of course, My Lord, of course. At once."

Tillit raised his hand. "What does a hero of the city have to do to ask a favor of the king?"

Xander smiled. "My apologies, old friend. For your bravery in saving the city, I would like to grant you any wish you desire that is within my power."

Tillit's mischievous eyes flickered to Renner and he stroked his clean, chubby chin. "Well, there is someone in the dungeon I'd like to get out. She was put there by your adviser here."

Renner's own eyes widened. "You do not mean to release Herbert!"

Xander smiled and bowed his head. "Then it shall be done. She will be released immediately."

Renner whipped his head to my lord. "B-but My Lord! She is a notorious fiend who-" Xander raised his hand.

"I am well aware of her misdeeds, and only ask that my friend here-" he looked to Tillit, "-ensures that she stays on her best behavior after her release."

Tillit grinned and gave Xander a sloppy salute. "I'll try my best, but I can't make any promises."

Xander chuckled. "I will take your word. Renner, please escort Tillit to the prisoner and release her."

"And Darda," I reminded him.

"But My Lord, you are not well and-"

"-and am perfectly capable of returning myself to the castle, but I expect my orders to be swifter than my feet," Xander warned him.

Renner's eyebrows crashed down and he shot a glare at Tillit. He spun on his heels away from us and stomped down the hall. Tillit gave us a wink before he climbed aboard one of the horses and followed the sullen adviser.

I turned back to my lord and jerked a thumb at Renner's retreating figure. "You'd better not leave me with that kind of babysitter again."

"I think someone means to grant you a different one, My Lady," Kinos spoke up as he nodded his head.

I expected a charge of red dragons, but it was merely to the church. A procession of the cloaked figures took us each in turn and offered us wet, warmed blankets. Some of them surrounded Xander and warmed his muscles to relax them.

I took one from a particularly tall fellow and wiped my face and chest of the muck. The result was the that white towel took on a very red tinge. I sheepishly smiled and held out the towel to him. "Sorry about that."

The hooded man took the towel, and I noticed his hands were unusually pale. "There is no need to worry, little niece. My order is pleased to help you."

I whipped my head up and looked with wide eyes at the face hidden in the shadow of the hood. A pair of bright blue eyes smiled back at me. He bowed his head and turned away.

I reached out for him, but Xander's voice called me back. "I would rather you not become lost again, Miriam," he teased.

I looked to him and pointed in the direction the figure walked. "But he's-" I turned in that direction. The man was gone. I dropped my arm to my side and frowned. "Where the heck did he go?"

Xander removed himself from the helpful hands of the men and looped an arm around my waist. "Your eyes tell me you have a story to tell me. Come, let us return to the castle so you can relate it to me."

CHAPTER 2

The return to the castle was a little slower than usual. Magnus's ship was still beached on the island, so we were forced to take a slower substitute ship. By the time we reached the castle I had related my story to Xander. His eyes shone with amazement as we stepped onto the dock.

He turned so we faced each other and grasped my hands. "You have certainly followed my orders to know the city with great enthusiasm."

"I'm just glad I got to know it before that red guy finished destroying it," I quipped.

He smiled and squeezed my hands. "As am I. I owe you a great deal of gratitude for your courage in facing such a relentless foe."

I grinned and shrugged. "All in a day's work for a Maiden."

A familiar face strode down the path from the castle. It was Darda, and a warm smile graced her lips. She walked up and bowed her head to me. "My Lady, I am glad to see you have returned."

I put my hands on my hips and looked her over with a teasing smile. "You're in the dungeon for a day and you've already forgotten my name?"

She raised her head. "My apologies, Miriam."

Xander set his hands on my elbows and pushed me toward Darda. "Darda, will you please escort your lady back to her chambers? I will be with you shortly."

I dug my heels in and looked over my shoulder at him. "Where are you going?"

"Your story has told me many things, and action is necessary on some of them," he told me.

I frowned. "I guess affairs of state is a reason. Not a goo one, but it's a reason. Just don't keep your Maiden waiting."

He smiled and bowed his head. "I swear it."

Darda and I walked up the path, leaving Xander to his work. My face fell as I looked over my companion. She was a little worn looking. "I'm sorry about getting you into that much trouble."

She shook her head. "It was my doing more than yours, Miriam." Her eyes flickered to me. "Am I wrong to assume you found the Library?"

I snorted and shook my head. "You wouldn't be wrong, but what I'd like to know is why everyone keeps telling me I was gone for a day when it only felt like a few minutes."

Darda looked ahead and furrowed her brow. "The Library is a strange place. It is said that time and place are changed to suit the needs of the one who finds their way to its hallowed balconies."

"So what you're saying is it sped up time for me?" I guessed.

She nodded. "I believe it did, but that is only a guess."

I shrugged. "It's as good a guess as any." I stopped in the hall and frowned.

Darda walked a few paces ahead before she half-turned to me. "Miriam?"

"You said you went there one time. What was your question?" I asked her.

She gazed at a nearby wall. "I, too, needed guidance in this fantastic world. My Lady-Cate-believed I would find out where I belonged at the Library."

"And did you?"

The corners of her lips curled up in a smile as she returned her attention to me. "Yes, and I have remained at the side of my ladies ever since."

I grinned. "Without regret?"

She bowed her head. "Without regret. Now we should be going."

We reached my chambers where I found an unwelcome surprise. A half dozen dresses were spread over the foot of the bed.

"I was informed they arrived late last night," Darda told me.

I walked up to them and picked up a lacy sleeve before I let it drop back to the bed. "Oh goody..."

The door opened and Xander walked in. Darda smiled at both of us before she bowed her head and left the room, closing the door behind her.

Xander walked over and settled his hands on my shoulders. His face grew long as his eyes looked into mine. "I am truly sorry for the horrors you had to go through."

I smiled and shook my head. "I already told you not to worry about it." I leaned back. "And speaking of trouble, what about that stuff in the south? Did you get that done and fly back here at supersonic speed?"

"I doubt I was at such a great speed as you imply, but Spiros is as fine an observer as myself. His report of the situation will be as though I was there," he told me. He looked past me at the dresses. A teasing smile slipped onto his lips. "I see your new attire has arrived."

My face fell. "Do I really have to wear these things?"

His lecherous eyes swept down my filthy dress. "I actually prefer you not to where anything at all."

I rolled my eyes. "Men. . ." An idea hit me and I grinned at him. "You know, you gave Tillit a reward for saving the day. I'd really like it if I didn't have to wear those things."

"Is that an official request?" he asked me.

I nodded. "Definitely, and with an added dose of pleading."

He chuckled. "Then I will grant your request, at least for the time being, though I do not believe you have any other clothing to wear."

I looked down at myself and cringed. "It's messy saving the day." My eyes flickered up to him. "And on that subject, did you learn anything about that red dragon guy?"

He shook his head. "No, and none of the sus survived the implosion of the chamber, but I hope some leads will-" There was a knock on the door. "Enter," Xander called.

LABYRINTH OF THE DRAGON

A soldier slipped inside and hurried up to us. He bowed his head. "Kumartua cannot be found, My Lord."

I wrinkled my nose. "Kumartua? The hunchback?"

"You don't think those sus and that red dragon knew their way around those tunnels by guessing, do you?" Tillit pointed out.

I shrugged. "I just thought they had a map."

He shook his head. "Nope. They had help, and that help was that conniving hunchback." He turned back to the soldier. "Search his personal belongings and notify the other kingdoms of his escape." The soldier bowed his head and left.

I looked to Xander and pursed my lips. "So there's still trouble?"

Xander faced me and smiled. "You have had your fill?"

"For a lifetime, at least a short one, which is what almost happened to me a half dozen times," I quipped.

He grasped my hands and chuckled. "After such an ordeal your fortitude to jest is amazing."

I snorted. "Who says I was joking?"

Xander slipped behind me and wrapped his arms over my chest and my back against his warm body. He leaned down and nuzzled my ear. "You would not wish to leave me so soon, would you, Miriam?"

I squirmed in his hold. "That's cheating."

He chuckled. "Then I would rather be a cheat than allow you to leave me."

I sighed and snuggled into his arms. "I'm not leaving-yet-but give me a couple months to recuperate."

Xander squeezed me. "I promise a few months reprieve."

At it turned out, that was a little longer promise than he could keep. But that's a story for another time.

A note from Mac

Thank you for purchasing my book! Your support means a lot to me, and I'm grateful to have the opportunity to entertain you with my stories.

If you'd like to continue reading the series, or wonder what else I might have up my writer's sleeve, feel free to check out my website at *macflynn.com*, or contact me at mac@macflynn.com.

* * *

Want to get an email when the next book is released? Sign up for the Wolf Den, the online newsletter with a bite, at *eepurl.com/tm-vn*!

Continue the adventure

Now that you've finished the book, feel free to check out my website at **macflynn.com** for the rest of the exciting series.

Here's also a little sneak-peek at the next book:

Traitors Among Dragons:

"Pull, My Lady, pull!"
"I'm pulling! I'm pulling!"
"You nearly have it, Miriam!"
"Give me some room!" I snapped.
There I was on the deck of the royal ship in the middle of the lake. It was three weeks after our adventures in the labyrinth, and I was taking some time to learn the intricacies of the cuisine. Behind me were Magnus and Darda, and in front of me was the wide expanse of waters. I held a fishing pole in my hands and determination on my face.
Magnus and Darda stepped back. I yanked back the fishing pole and spun another few feet of horse-hair line around the hook at the base of the wooden stick. The stick bent over the railing and brushed the waves that rocked the ship. A silver fish broke the surface and sailed over the waves before it splashed back into the water. I gritted my teeth and gave a hard pull of the rod with both hands.
The fish flew out of the water and landed with a hard slap onto the deck of the ship. It flopped about

before Magnus threw a net over the flopping behemoth. Its large silver belly shimmered in the warm afternoon sun.

Magnus stepped up and grinned over my prey. "A nice one, My Lady. A good two pygme, if Ah'm not a daktylos off. The god of the lake smiles on you."

I blinked at him before I looked to Darda. "Is that good?"

She smiled and nodded. "The measurement is nearly equal to thirty inches."

I straightened and grinned. "That's good enough for me."

Magnus nodded. "Aye, tis a good fish. My Lord and ya will eat well tonight."

I turned away at the glistening castle set against the hillside. It was a glistening crown to the large white city at my back. The spires cast their long shadows over the rippling waters of the large lake that separated the capital from the residence of its lord, Xander, and its beautiful, majestic lady, namely me.

A soft smile slipped onto my lips. "Let's see that dragon eat this all by himself."

The old captain chuckled. "Ah won't be counting my cargo the ship's come to port, My Lady." He looked over his shoulder at the helm. Nimeni, his pale first mate, stood behind the wheel. "Back to the castle!"

Nimeni nodded and aimed the bow to the castle. We sailed over the deep blue waters of Lake Beriadan and toward the long dock of the castle. I set my hands on the railing and looked into the water. My distorted reflection stared back at me, but far below that was a band of blue light that flitted alongside the boat. I grinned and waved. It flicked its tail before it dove into the black depths of the deep lake.

We arrived at the dock, and my catch and I were escorted into the castle. My dragon lord, the annoyingly handsome Xander, met us in the courtyard. His eyes immediately fell on the fish in the arms of the castle guard. "The gods were kind to you this day."

"I only needed one, and a little skill," I told him.

He smiled. "An unfortunate combination for the fish. Shall we consume it tonight?"

I grinned. "I was thinking about parading it around a little longer, but-" I pinched my nose shut, "-I think it's already starting to smell."

Xander chuckled as he nodded at the guard who left us. "Then we will feast tonight, and enjoy one another's company later in the evening."

I sidled up to him and leaned against him. "Are you sure you can make time in your busy kingdom-running schedule for me?" His face fell. I winced. "Bad news?"

He wrapped his arm around my waist and shook his head. "No, something far worse."

My heart dropped into my stomach as I looked into his crestfallen face. "You're going away again?"

Xander turned to me and clasped my hands. A smile teased the corners of his lips. "No, my Miriam. Bucephalus and I will not leave your side for a long while yet. What concerns me is the Bestia that attacked you, and the raid on the south."

I arched an eyebrow. "You think they're connected?"

He nodded. "I do. The raid led me away from my city when it most needed me, and the Bestia who attacked the south took nothing of value from the poor villages. Thus we may assume they meant for me not to be present during their search for Bucephalus."

I grinned. "But I was."

Xander leaned forward and pecked a teasing kiss on my lips. He leaned back and studied my eyes with a true smile. "Yes, and I owe you my city for it."

"How about just saving me a piece of that fish?" I teased.

Xander straightened and bowed his head. "I will do as you command, and more."

As it turned out he couldn't keep his promise, but that wasn't his fault. The supper hour came, a late one at seven o'clock. Xander and I sat at the long table in the large dining hall with a row of servants standing at the ready should we need another fork or a bib. I was seated on his left and in front of us was a fortune's worth of silverware. The silver fish was presented to us on a silver platter.

Xander picked up his fork and knife, and smiled at me. "May I offer you a fin, or perhaps the tail?"

I snorted. "You really like to eat like a king here, don't you?"

He chuckled as he carved a hearty portion from the fish and slid it onto my plate. "It is the company that gives me such an appetite, and the nightly exercise."

I picked up my own utensils and sliced into the fish. I held up the slice and grinned at him over the piece. "You could say you caught yourself a perfect Maiden."

Xander placed a large slice on his plate and grinned. "And I have you as proof my victory was not a fish story."

Our tug-of-war with puns ended with the entrance of Tillit. The sus sauntered into the room and took for himself the chair opposite me. "Good evening, my favorite dragon lord and Maiden."

Xander arched an eyebrow as he studied our unexpected guest. "You did not bribe the guards to allow you entrance again, did you?"

Tillit grinned as he shook his head. "Nope. I'm actually here on official business." He reached into his coat and drew out an envelope which he held out to Xander. "I was with Kinos when this came up to the front gate. They were swamped out there-you really need to add another gate-so he asked me to give it to you."

Xander took the envelope and opened it while Tillit looked at the fish on my plate. "It looks like Beriadan's still rewarding you for saving his city."

I frowned and wagged my knife at him. "There was some skill involved, too."

He chuckled, but the mirth died on his lips when he glanced at Xander's strained face. "No good news from the Heavy Mountains?"

Xander shook his head as he broached the contents of the letter again. "No. On the contrary, Herod wishes for my assistance, and that I travel to his realm immediately."

Tillit gave off a piggish snort. "If that's true it'll be the first time that prince of darkness asks anyone for help. What's he want help with, anyway?"

"He does not say."

The sus wrinkled his flat nose. "Typical. That guy's more paranoid than any sus I've met, and that's saying something."

Xander folded the note and slipped it back into the envelope before he looked to me. "I fear this will call me away again."

My eyebrows crashed down. "Just you?"

"I did promise you rest for at least a month," he reminded me.

I set my elbow on the table and leaned toward him to look him square in the eyes. "Let's just get this straight: from now on where you go, I go. If there's going to be trouble, I can at least scream so you can fly down and rescue your damsel."

"Can you not whistle?" he wondered.

I snorted. "I can't even breathe through my nose."

He pressed his lips together and gave off a melodious sound. "It is easy."

I leaned back in my chair and folded my arms over my chest. "Not easy enough for me to do it, and I'm kind of hoping I'm not even going to need to scream on this little adventure of ours."

"I will have to teach you some time," he replied as he turned to Tillit. "Can we expect the pleasure of your company on this adventure?"

Tillit stood and shook his head. "This is one adventure I'm staying out of. There's only room enough on that mountain for one sus, and that position's filled. Besides, I've got some business at Bear Bay that might prove lucrative." He turned away, but paused and looked over his shoulder at us. His expression was tense. "Whatever you do up there on that god-forsaken place, just don't get lost. I wouldn't want my best customers bleaching their bones among those stupid rocks."

Xander smiled and bowed his head. "I swear nothing of the sort will happen."

Tillit grinned. "Well, that's better than nothing. Good luck on your trip up that lonely mountain." He strolled from the room, but a wisp of his voice floated behind him. "You're gonna need it. . ."

My eyes flickered to Xander and I jerked my head in the direction Tillit had gone. "Are we going to need it?"

Xander took up his knife and fork and sliced into his fish. "Perhaps," he replied as he took a bite.

My face fell. "That doesn't exactly give me comfort."

His eyes looked up from his plate. "Would you rather remain behind?"

I frowned and slumped in my chair. "No, but still-" I couldn't organize my worried thoughts.

Xander set down his utensils and took one of my hands in his. He gave it a gentle squeeze as he smiled at me. "Have I allowed any harm to come to you?"

I furrowed my brow. "Well, now that you mention it there was that one time at the Portal-"

"You returned to me unscathed."

"-and the near-death experience at the ruins in the forest-"

"Death did not even part us."

"-and then you left me to protect the city all by myself-"

Xander leaned forward and pressed a passionate kiss on my lips that heated my body. I groaned into the union and whimpered when he pulled us apart. A mischievous smile slipped onto his lips. "You were saying?"

I glared at him. "I was saying that you play dirty in arguments."

He leaned back in his chair and smiled gently at me. "However devious my actions, know that my intentions toward you will forever me pure."

My shoulders slumped and I sighed. "All right, I'll rehire you as my bodyguard, but don't expect any bonuses while we're there." I furrowed my brow. "And where exactly is 'there,' anyway? And who are we helping exactly?"

"Herod is the dragon lord of the Heavy Mountains, a realm located in the northeastern part of the continent." He looked down at the envelope that lay beside his plate. "It would be a rather long journey on horse, but the urgency of his letter implies we should fly."

I raised an eyebrow. "Like full-dragon fly?"

He shook his head. "No. Though that form is faster in flight, the distance is fully two days away by air. Any in our entourage who is not a lord would perish from the strain on their bodies."

I winced. "Only a day? How long would it take you to-well, you know-"

"Two days before my body, too, would give out," he told me.

"But weren't you guys dragons before? I mean, you haven't always been human looking, have you?" I asked him.

He shook his head. "No, but the days of flight in our dragon bodies are long past. Those with the greatest strength of dragon form perished long ago in wars against the humans and each other. The lines that remain are too weak to retain the form without certain death."

My face fell. "Bummer."

Xander smiled at me. "Do not pity us. We still have our wings, and they grant us enough freedom to travel over the continent without too much difficulty. We should arrive at the border of Herod's realm within three days."

"Sounds like the usual terrifying fun. When do we leave?"

"At first light."

Other series by Mac Flynn

Contemporary Romance
Being Me
Billionaire Seeking Bride
The Family Business
Loving Places
PALE Series
Trapped In Temptation

Demon Romance
Ensnare: The Librarian's Lover
Ensnare: The Passenger's Pleasure
Incubus Among Us
Lovers of Legend
Office Duties
Sensual Sweets
Unnatural Lover

Dragon Romance
Maiden to the Dragon

Ghost Romance
Phantom Touch

Vampire Romance
Blood Thief
Blood Treasure
Vampire Dead-tective
Vampire Soul

Werewolf Romance
Alpha Blood
Alpha Mated
Beast Billionaire
By My Light
Desired By the Wolf
Falling For A Wolf
Garden of the Wolf
Highland Moon
In the Loup
Luna Proxy
Marked By the Wolf
Moon Chosen
Continued on next page
Moon Lovers
Oracle of Spirits
Scent of Scotland: Lord of Moray
Shadow of the Moon
Sweet & Sour
Wolf Lake

Manufactured by Amazon.ca
Bolton, ON